It slammed into him like a tornado.

Desire.

Then Maggie licked her lips and he did the only thing he could.

He kissed her. And it was perfect.

Until she slapped him.

"Oh, no," she said, her finger stabbing his chest. "You don't get to do this, Griffin Stone. You rejected me."

He'd seen many sides of Maggie, but never had he seen her so angry.

He wrapped his fingers around hers. "I'm sorry. I didn't mean to."

"I've moved on," she announced, yanking her hand from his. "Just like you."

The words stung. How could he tell her he still wanted her? He was as messed up as he'd been four months ago. Their past was messy, the present just as complicated.

Why had he pulled her away from the festival in the first place? If he'd been thinking about anything other than how much he missed her, he would've known that was a horrible idea.

But that was the problem. Maggie was all he could think of anymore.

So what was he going to do about it?

Part Two of Maggie and Griffin's love story!

Dear Reader,

Second-chance romances are my favorites so this story was so much fun to write. Thank you for joining me as Maggie and Griffin continue on their winding road to happily-ever-after.

In *Second Chance in Stonecreek*, Maggie has to dig in and find a strength she didn't realize she had, both to win the mayoral election and to see her younger sister through some troubled times. She discovers what's really important to her—and that includes both her family and Griffin Stone.

Griffin definitely hadn't expected to fall for Maggie, but now he has to take a chance on opening his guarded heart in order to convince her to give him another shot.

Love is never easy, but it's always worth it in the end. I hope you love this story and don't forget to check out the final book in the series next month, *A Stonecreek Christmas Reunion*.

I'd love to hear from you at www.michellemajor.com or connect with me on Facebook or Twitter.

Happy reading,

Michelle

Second Chance in Stonecreek

—

Michelle Major

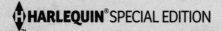

HHARLEQUIN®SPECIAL EDITION

Recycling programs
for this product may
not exist in your area.

ISBN-13: 978-1-335-46604-4

Second Chance in Stonecreek

Printed in U.S.A.

Michelle Major grew up in Ohio but dreamed of living in the mountains. Soon after graduating with a degree in journalism, she pointed her car west and settled in Colorado. Her life and house are filled with one great husband, two beautiful kids, a few furry pets and several well-behaved reptiles. She's grateful to have found her passion writing stories with happy endings. Michelle loves to hear from her readers at michellemajor.com.

Visit the Author Profile page
at Harlequin.com for more titles.

To everyone at Harlequin—thank you for making the stories I write into real books. I'm so grateful.

Chapter One

"It won't do for people to see you staring off into space like you're high on the wacky weed or something."

Maggie Spencer blinked, then turned to her seventy-nine-year-old grandmother. "Grammy, did you just use the term 'wacky weed'?"

"I'm not as behind the times as you seem to believe," Vivian Spencer shot back, adjusting the collar of her Jackie O–inspired tweed coat. "I know what's going on with teens today."

"I'm twenty-seven," Maggie pointed out. A gentle autumn breeze whistled across the town square in Stonecreek, Oregon, her beloved hometown. She pushed away a lock of hair that had blown into her face. "I don't smoke pot or anything else. You know that."

She waved to Rob Frisbie, who owned the local grocery store, walking past on his way to the beer booth. How Maggie would have liked to join him at the moment.

"You could eat it," her grandmother suggested tartly. "That's a thing, you know."

"I know," Maggie answered, struggling to keep her smile in place as she greeted a couple that approached her information booth, neither of whom she recognized. "Welcome to Fall Fest," she said brightly. "Are you visiting for the afternoon?"

"We drove down from Portland," the woman offered as both she and the man at her side nodded. "We're doing a wine tasting at Harvest Vineyards later this afternoon."

"We're glad you stopped by the festival," Maggie said. "I'm Maggie Spencer, Stonecreek's mayor." She picked up a tourism pamphlet and one of the flyers she'd printed for the annual festival. "Here's some information on things to do around town and a list of the activities happening today. If you have five vendors stamp your flyer, bring it back, then you'll be entered to win a weekend stay at our own local Miriam Inn."

The woman smiled and took the papers as Grammy said, "I'm Vivian Spencer, Maggie's grandmother and former mayor." She leaned forward as if imparting a great secret. "She's up for reelection next month. It's a surprisingly tight race given that she inherited the position. I held it for almost a decade with barely any opposition."

Heat rose to Maggie's cheeks as the woman's smile turned awkward. "Well, good luck, then," she said and hurried away with her husband.

"I didn't inherit the position," Maggie said through clenched teeth. "I was elected and I've done well during my first term."

"Don't take that tone with me." Vivian patted her silver hair, which was swept into a neat chignon on the back of her head. "Is it any wonder I question whether you're on drugs with how you've been acting lately?"

"I'm not taking a tone," Maggie said, making her voice gentle. "Or doing drugs. The campaign is going fine."

"Fine isn't enough to win the election." Vivian reached out a crepey hand to squeeze Maggie's arm. "I want this for you, Mary Margaret. It's your destiny."

Maggie sighed. Being the mayor of Stonecreek wasn't exactly on par with a lightning bolt scar on her forehead, but she loved her town and her role as mayor. Her grandmother meant well. Grammy had stepped in to help raise Maggie and her siblings when their mother died almost twelve years ago. Maggie's father, Jim, had struggled with being a single dad of three children. Grammy had been a constant source of love and support, and if she was a trifle overbearing and autocratic, Maggie could deal with it.

After all, she'd been content to let her grandmother steer the ship for years. It was only in the past few months that Maggie had finally wanted out from under Grammy's manicured thumb.

"I want it, too," Maggie said, wrapping an arm around Grammy's shoulders. "Plans for the debate are going well. We have lots of volunteers on the campaign."

"Debate." Vivian sniffed. "I still cannot believe Jason Stone challenged to you to a public debate. It's undignified."

Maggie stifled a laugh. "It's politics, Grammy."

"Not in Stonecreek." Her grandmother straightened the already neat stacks of pamphlets on the table in front of them. "Spencers have held the position of mayor for decades in this town. Your great-great-uncle and then your grandfather—rest his soul—and then me. For Jason to think he has a right to challenge you is preposterous."

"Why do people say 'rest his or her soul' when talking about a dead person?" Maggie asked, grasping for any way to change the subject before her grandmother latched onto—

"I have no doubt that upstart will make an issue of your wedding, or lack thereof." Grammy gave a quelling look, ignoring Maggie's off-topic question. "You wouldn't be in this predicament if you'd married Trevor Stone."

"You're right," Maggie agreed, keeping her tone even. What her grandmother didn't know was that she'd found Trevor cheating on her minutes before she was supposed to walk down the aisle. So there was a good chance she'd be in another predicament entirely. "I guess it was his loss."

Grammy sniffed again. "Stupid boy."

"He's a grown man," Maggie countered, "although I'm with you on the stupid part."

"No better than he should be," Vivian muttered.

"Another saying I don't under—"

"Although still a better option than that brother of his."

Maggie's chest tightened at the mention of Griffin Stone. The prodigal son of the Stone family had returned to Stonecreek for the wedding and ended up rescuing Maggie when she'd fled the church after discovering her fiancé's betrayal. They'd struck up an unlikely friendship and so much more from Maggie's point of view. But her romance with Griffin had been short-lived.

He was still in town, once again rebuilding the tasting room at his family's successful vineyard after fire had ravaged part of it for a second time in as many decades. Only, Maggie's sixteen-year-old sister, Morgan, had caused the fire at the beginning of summer. The fallout of that tragic accident plus the tension that existed between the Stones and Spencers, fueled by a rivalry that dated back to the founding of the town, had driven a wedge between Griffin and Maggie that she had no idea how to combat.

And Griffin hadn't even wanted to try. That was how little she'd meant to him.

Megan Roe, the town's version of a girl Friday, approached the booth. "Hey, Maggie," she called. "Hi, Mrs. Spencer. I'm here for my shift."

Megan was in her early twenties and had grown up in Stonecreek, just like Maggie. In fact, she'd babysat the three Roe sisters through most of high school. As mayor, one of Maggie's biggest concerns was attracting young people to the town. She wanted to keep things current and make sure there were good jobs to be found in Stonecreek so the town stayed relevant. Harvest Vineyards brought in tourists, but they also needed a strong foundation of other businesses to keep the local economy strong.

Grammy looked the young woman up and down. "Is that what you're wearing to represent this town?" she asked, disapproval clear in her tone.

Luckily, Megan didn't seem to notice. "Yeah." She pulled at the hem of her minidress, which looked like an overlong flannel shirt with a red-and-black-checkered pattern. Her heavily highlighted hair was down around her shoulders and she wore black ankle boots with a chunky heel. "I got it last week when my sister and I went shopping in Portland. There are so many cool stores in the city. Around here, it's online shopping or nothing."

"Next time try nothi—"

"You look great," Maggie interrupted her grandmother, gently pushing her from behind the booth. "Thanks for volunteering. We've had a steady stream of people stop by. Entries for the night on the town giveaway are starting to roll in. It should pick up before the band starts in an hour."

"No problem," Megan said with a smile. "My boyfriend is coming by to keep me company."

Maggie squeezed Grammy's elbow when the older woman tsk-tsked. "I'll be around for a bit. Text if you need anything."

The woman waved as Maggie ushered her grandma away from the booth.

"She looks like an unwashed vagrant," Vivian said, wrinkling her nose.

"She's stylish," Maggie countered.

"Dirty hobo is a style now?"

"Grammy, don't be mean. Megan is great and it was nice of her to volunteer."

"I'm not mean. I'm honest. That girl could benefit from some constructive criticism. Did you see how short her skirt was? If she bends over, everyone will see her—"

"She looks fine." Maggie shook her head. "You can't worry about every little thing, Grammy. You've retired. The town isn't your responsibility anymore."

Vivian clasped a hand to her chest, her index finger gliding up to the pearl necklace she'd worn since Maggie could remember. "You're going to break my heart with that kind of talk, Mary Margaret. You know this town means everything to me."

"I know," Maggie whispered, hugging her grandmother. She hated feeling at odds with anyone, especially Grammy, who Maggie loved with her whole heart. But Vivian Spencer was part of the old guard, with ideas and plans for the town that didn't necessarily benefit the diversity and enterprise Maggie wanted Stonecreek to be known for. She had to find a way to minimize her grandmother's influence while still showing the older woman the respect she deserved. "I love you, Grammy."

"You, too, sweetheart." Vivian drew back. "I'm going to head home. I'll see you tomorrow for Sunday dinner?"

"Of course."

Maggie watched her grandmother walk away, then turned for the bustling town square. Booths lined the perimeter with local artisans selling jewelry and gifts and local restaurants serving a variety of tasting options. Maggie had put in countless hours with the festival committee to make this year's Fall Fest a success.

Despite what she'd told her grandma, she did have concerns about the upcoming election. Jason Stone had been running a subtle smear campaign, a portion of it reflecting on her decision to walk away from her wedding without outing Trevor as the rat fink cheater he was.

But the more insidious digs at her came from her relationship with her grandmother. Her opponent was insinuating exactly what Grammy had just stated out loud: that Maggie had been elected because of nepotism and not on her own merits. She hated giving any credence to the idea, but the doubts pinging through her head made it even more essential that she win the election.

She sighed and started forward toward the bustling midway. Unfortunately right now, schmoozing and socializing seemed about as appealing as downing a bowl of cockroaches. Maggie was working overtime on the overtime she normally put in to prove her dedication to her job. She was tired, so the thought of making small talk for a couple of hours had her stomach tightening.

"You look like you're walking into a gathering of flesh-eating zombies," a voice called from behind her.

She turned to see her best friend, Brenna Apria, and Brenna's young daughter, Ellie, walking toward her.

"All zombies eat flesh," Ellie announced as they got closer.

"Aren't you too young to know that, squirt?" Maggie asked, crouching down and holding her arms wide. Ellie ran forward, wrapping her thin arms around Maggie's neck.

"I'm either going to be a zombie or a vampire cheerleader for Halloween," Ellie told her matter-of-factly, "so I'm doing research on both of them."

"She loves to be scared." Brenna gave a mock shudder. "I don't know where she gets it."

"Marcus and I watched *Gremlins* last weekend," Ellie reported. "It was PG but still Mommy had to cover her eyes for the scary parts."

"How is Marcus?" Maggie lifted a brow in Brenna's direction.

Her friend tried to hide the enamored smile that curved her mouth. "He's good. Things are getting back to normal after harvest season at the vineyard."

"Harvest season," Maggie murmured. That meant all hands on deck at the vineyard, although the winery also stayed open. Each year, Brenna coordinated grape-stomping competitions and the opportunity for the public to pick grapes in designated vineyards. But Maggie had not gone to any of the community events this year. It was too difficult to be near Griffin, which was stupid and possibly pathetic on her part.

Although she'd known him her whole life, he'd been a jerk as a kid and all through high school, three years older than her and definitely not interested in a rule follower like Maggie.

That had changed, to her great surprise, when he'd returned to Stonecreek. Even so, they'd only been friends for a few weeks and spent one blissful night together before her little fairy tale had come crashing down. Or maybe she'd just imagined their powerful connection.

The great sex had been a real thing. She hadn't made that up. Everything else... Well, she always did have a vivid imagination.

"You okay?" Brenna asked, her brow furrowing.

"Just tired." Maggie forced a smile. "Not really up for doing the mayoral thing tonight."

"You're welcome to hang with us," her friend offered.

"Come with us," Ellie shouted, grabbing her hand. "We're going to get apple cider and kettle corn and have our faces painted."

The warmth of the girl's fingers wrapped around hers made the band of tension wrapped around Maggie's stomach ease ever so slightly.

"It's a real girls' night out," Brenna added with a smile at her daughter.

"Then count me in," Maggie said.

They headed into the square, stopping at each booth. With Brenna and Ellie flanking either side of her, Maggie was able to relax, greeting old friends and various townspeople and remembering why she worked so hard at her job.

She loved this little corner of the Willamette Valley, from the terra-cotta and classical revival-style buildings to the bright yellows and golds of the leaves in the fall.

"At least I'm not getting a ton of side-eye anymore," Maggie said to Brenna as they stood a few feet from the face-painting booth, waiting for Ellie to be transformed into a Bengal tiger.

Brenna toasted her cider cup against Maggie's. "I told you all they needed was time. People were a little shocked that you walked away from the wedding, but that doesn't change what you mean to this town."

"There are still a few who haven't forgiven me." Maggie lifted a finger to touch the small butterfly one of the teenagers working the face-painting station had drawn onto her cheek. Ellie had insisted Maggie get her face done before the girl would agree to sit. "My grandmother might be one of them."

Brenna made a face. "I can't help you there. Oh, no. Don't turn around."

Maggie immediately looked over her shoulder to see Griffin walking toward them, an unfamiliar woman at his side. The woman was beautiful, with flowing, raven-colored hair, a fashion-model-thin frame and long legs tucked into vintage cowboy boots. She wore a baggy dress that just grazed her thighs, but the shape of a dress didn't matter when a woman looked like that. Griffin towered over her and was leaning close as the woman gazed up at him.

Maggie's heart stuttered.

No, they weren't heading toward her. The two of them were so engrossed in each other they could have been walking on a deserted street for all they noticed the crowd around them.

Until Griffin looked up. His green gaze caught on Maggie, the heat from it like being stabbed with a hot poker.

"What part of 'don't turn around' confused you?" Brenna muttered under her breath.

"It's fine," Maggie said, her voice weak as she faced forward again. "Who is she?"

"Maggie?"

Heat pooled low in her belly at the sound of Griffin's rich baritone. Pathetic. She was the most pathetic woman on the planet. This man had rejected her four months ago. She had no reason to be twitter-pated over him. She had no reason to feel anything for him.

To borrow from one of Maggie's favorite old-school pop songs, tell that to her heart.

But she spun around, pasting a bright smile on her face. "Hey, Griffin. How's it hang—"

She yelped when Brenna pinched the back of her arm. Hard.

"Hey," Griffin said slowly, darting a dubious glance between the two of them. "I'm...um...doing fine. How are you?"

"Hunky-dory," she said, then inwardly cringed as Brenna groaned. "I'm fine, too," she amended, her cheeks feeling like they'd just caught fire. "Fine."

"Great." Griffin nodded and she watched his throat bob as he swallowed. "I wanted to introduce you to an old friend." He indicated the woman standing next to him. "This is Cassie Barlow. Cassie's an interior designer up in Seattle. We've worked on a few projects together over the years."

Is that what the kids are calling it now? Maggie thought to herself. She held out a hand, her cheeks aching from the perma-grin plastered across her face. "Nice to meet you."

"You, too," the woman said, her eyes bright. "Great butterfly."

Seriously, could cheek muscles grow so hard they cracked? "I had my face painted," Maggie said, then sighed. Master of the obvious. How charming.

"My daughter demanded it," Brenna offered quickly. "Maggie did it for Ellie."

Griffin introduced Brenna to Cassie and then Cassie turned to Maggie again. "Grif tells me you're mayor of this town."

Grif. She called him Grif. Oh, yeah. They worked

together. Worked together on getting busy, most likely.

Maggie blinked when she realized everyone was staring at her. "Yes, mayor," she agreed like an imbecile. "I'm mayor."

Cassie tilted her head and Maggie thought the other woman must think her the biggest ninny she'd ever met. But Cassie's eyes remained kind. It was ridiculously difficult to hate someone with such kind eyes.

Ellie ran up to Brenna at that moment, her face painted in black and orange stripes. The girl held up her hands like claws and growled at her mom, then turned to Maggie and roared loudly.

"I'm ferocious," she announced.

Maggie cowered in mock fear, never so grateful for the interruption. "Oh, scary tiger," she said, making her voice tremble. "Have mercy on this little butterfly."

"You're too tiny for me to eat," Ellie said with a nod. "I better go get a corn dog."

Maggie grinned, then looked up at Griffin and Cassie. "You heard the tiger. We've got to feed her before she starves."

"It was lovely to meet you," Cassie said softly.

"You, too," Maggie agreed. She gave a casual wave. "See you around, *Grif*."

Griffin gave a sharp nod but didn't respond.

And even though Maggie wanted nothing more than to escape this awkward interaction, she couldn't quite force her legs to walk away from him until Ellie took her hand and tugged.

Chapter Two

"She thinks we're together," Cassie murmured as Maggie disappeared into the crowd milling about the town square.

"We are together." Griffin unclenched his hands, which had ended up fisted at his sides, and concentrated on keeping his expression neutral. It took every bit of willpower he possessed to watch Maggie turn away. He wanted to reach for her, to pull her close and bury his face in her hair, breathing in her flowery scent.

"As in we're dating." Cassie rolled her eyes.

"We're not dating," Griffin said as if his old friend needed clarification. "We haven't dated for years."

Cassie smacked him hard on the shoulder. "I know that, you idiot. Your Maggie doesn't."

"She's not mine," he muttered, shoving his hands into his pockets. He continued to stare in the direction Maggie had walked. Every few seconds he'd get a glimpse of her caramel-colored hair or a flash of the bright butterfly painted on her cheek as she turned to say something to Brenna. This was the first time he'd seen her since he'd ended what was between them. Ended it before it had really had a chance to start.

Stonecreek was a small town and, as mayor, Maggie was a very visible resident. He'd holed up at the vineyard for most of the summer, repairing the damage to the tasting room from the fire that Maggie's sister had accidentally started when her plans for teenage seduction had gone awry.

Cole Maren, the boy Morgan Spencer had set her sights on that night, had worked tirelessly at Griffin's side. Despite the kid's past and less-than-desirable family situation, Cole seemed determined to stay on the right track. Griffin wished he'd made that choice when he was younger. It had taken him years of running from the stupidity of his youth to straighten out his mind and soul.

A weight settled in his chest like a lead balloon as he watched Maggie and he wondered how successful he'd actually been.

"You look at each other," Cassie said, moving toward a vendor selling handmade soaps and lotions, "like you belong together."

"You don't understand how it is in Stonecreek," Griffin said with a sigh.

Cassie dabbed a sample of lemon-scented lotion on her hands, turning to Griffin as she rubbed it into her skin. "What's there to understand? You care about her. She cares about you. All that other family history stuff is just noise. It doesn't have to matter, Grif. Trust me. I'm all about cutting away things that don't matter these days."

Griffin opened his mouth to argue, then shut it again. Cassie had paid this unexpected visit to him to share that she'd been diagnosed with a brain tumor. She was due to start treatment in Seattle in a couple of days and said the doctors had given her a great prognosis. But the news had changed her—maybe for the better—as she seemed at peace in a way he hadn't ever known her to be.

"You have to try," Cassie urged.

He glanced beyond her and spotted Maggie talking to a tall guy who looked to be in his midthirties. Brenna stood a few feet away watching Ellie play in the bouncy house, like she was trying to give Maggie and the stranger space. The man handed Maggie his phone and she punched something into it. Her number, Griffin assumed, and felt adrenaline stab his gut.

"Give me a few minutes," he told his friend, earning a wide smile.

"I'll meet you in front of the stage," Cassie agreed. "The band is starting in a few minutes."

He nodded and headed in Maggie's direction, absently waving to the people who called out greetings.

"We need to talk," he told her, moving to stand between her and the man.

Her fine brows furrowed. "I don't think so."

"Come on, Maggie," he coaxed. "It won't take long."

"Everything okay?" the stranger asked.

Maggie looked around Griffin and smiled at the man. "Just a little bit of bothersome town business."

Griffin felt his eyes narrow.

"It was nice meeting you, James," she said sweetly.

"I'll call you next week," the man answered, and Griffin's hand itched to deck the guy.

Maggie held up her index finger to someone behind

Griffin—Brenna, he guessed—then looked up at him, her gray eyes cool. "So talk."

"Not here." Before she could protest, he circled her wrist with his hand and led her away from the crowd.

"Is this necessary?" she asked tartly.

"You sound like your grandma when you use that snippy tone," he said, flashing a smile at her.

She glared in return.

He continued to the edge of the park that took up one full square block in the middle of downtown Stonecreek and moved around the side of the town hall building.

"Griffin, what are you doing?" She dug in her heels and tugged her wrist from his grasp.

He turned and could see the freckles that sprinkled her nose and upper cheeks and the bits of gold around the edges of her eyes. He smelled the light scent of her shampoo and damn if he didn't want to press his face into the crook of her neck. As much as he thought he had his feelings under control, the reality of this moment still slammed through him with the force of a tornado.

Then she licked her lips and it was too much. All of it. The return to Stonecreek, the acrimony he couldn't manage to fix with Trevor, their mother's expectations and the constant undercurrent of his past mistakes that seemed to follow him everywhere, trailing behind like a child's blanket.

He did the only thing he could think of in the moment.

He pressed his lips to Maggie's mouth. It was perfect. Her softness, the sweet taste of apples, the feel of her body so close to him. All of it perfect.

Until she slapped him.

She shook out her hand, seeming as shocked by her reaction as he was. His cheek stung, although he figured he deserved that snap of pain and so much more.

"You kissed me." The words were an accusation and he had the good sense to realize how out of line he'd been.

"I'm sorry." He ran a hand through his hair. "It seemed like a good idea at the time."

She made a noise in the back of her throat that might have been a growl. "Are you crazy?"

"About you?" He flashed a smile. "Yeah. Yeah, I— Oof." He stumbled when she pushed on his chest. Hard.

"No, no, no," she said, her voice low, almost a snarl. Each exclamation was punctuated with another shove. "You don't get to do this, Griffin Stone."

He'd seen many sides of Maggie, but never had he seen her so angry. Color stained her cheeks and her breath was coming out in ragged puffs. "I'm not—"

"You rejected me." She jabbed one finger into his chest. "You said horrible things about my sister and my family."

"I was angry." He wrapped his fingers around hers, pulled it away from his body. "I'm sorry. I didn't mean—"

"I've moved on," she announced, yanking her hand from his. "Just like you."

"Like me?"

"The woman you introduced me to. The one who calls you Grif. Oh, Grif…" She gave an overly girlish laugh. "You're so handsome, Grif. So strong, Grif. Oh, Griffy-poo."

"Cassie has never called me 'Griffy-poo' in her life."

"Not the point," Maggie ground out.

Right. What was the point? Why had he pulled her away from the festival in the first place? It certainly hadn't been to kiss her. If he'd been thinking about anything other than how much he missed her, he would have known that was a horrible idea.

He'd wanted to talk to her about Cassie. She'd misinterpreted and—

"I'm dating someone."

The statement jolted him back to the present moment.

"No." The word came out as a puff of breath.

Her eyes narrowed again. "Yes. Well, not yet exactly. I'm going to date someone."

"Hypothetically?" he demanded, feeling a muscle tick in his jaw. "Or in real life?"

"Real life. The man you saw." She paused as if searching for a detail she'd forgotten. "James. He's a doctor."

"Bully for him."

"For both of us," she agreed. "I met him working on the hospital fund-raiser."

"The one I'm hosting at the tasting room?"

"Your mother is the official host," she pointed out, not very helpfully in his opinion.

"It's my vineyard."

"Your family's vin—"

"You know what I mean," he interrupted.

"I know…" She blew out a long breath. "We are

not together. Your choice, Griffin. Has something changed?"

Panic spiked through him. He wanted to say yes, but it wasn't true. He was as messed up as he'd been four months ago. Their past was messy, the present just as complicated. He'd told her he didn't do complicated. He'd hurt her. The pain he'd caused still reflected in her gaze and he hated himself for it.

He'd grown so damn tired of hating himself.

"I'm sorry," he said again, then shook his head.

She gave him a sad smile. "So many apologies between us."

"I want it to be different." As if that mattered when he was too much of a coward to do anything about it.

The smile faded from her face. "Me, too."

"Maggie—"

"I need to get back to the festival." She straightened her fitted red turtleneck sweater. The bottom edge of the butterfly on her cheek had smeared slightly where his thumb had grazed her face. "Brenna will be wondering about me."

He nodded. "Have a good night, Maggie May."

She tucked a lock of hair behind her ear, a small diamond stud glimmering in her lobe. She had beautiful ears. Every inch of her was beautiful to him.

"Have fun with Cassie," she said, then whirled and hurried away.

He wanted to call after her, to explain there was nothing between him and his ex-girlfriend. But what good would that do? Would it change everything that prevented him from committing to Maggie?

No. It felt like nothing ever changed in Stonecreek.

Cassie had told him the noise around them didn't matter, but it was all Griffin could hear, drowning out even the beat of his own heart.

Morgan Spencer shoved her phone into the top drawer of her desk when she heard her father's footsteps on the creaky staircase of the house where she'd been born. Literally born in the bathtub down the hall.

This home and town were all she'd ever known. Her perfect life and her perfect family and she didn't fit in at all.

There was a soft knock on the door and then her dad entered.

"Hey, Mo-Mo. No Fall Fest for you this year?"

She rolled her eyes. "I'm grounded. Remember?"

Her father grimaced, looking slightly sheepish. "Of course. I remember. Fire at Harvest Vineyards. You and a toppled candle."

"It was an accident," she said, shame pulsing through her at the reminder of her stupidity.

"I understand, but there are still consequences to your actions, young lady."

"I'm not so young," she shot back.

"You're sixteen."

"Duh. It's a wonder you even remember."

"Attitude isn't going to help, Morgan." Her dad's tone had turned abnormally disapproving. Jim Spencer was a big man. At fifty-one, his shoulders remained broad and only a sprinkling of silver darted his thick brown hair. Tonight he wore faded jeans and a ratty sweatshirt. From the earthy scent emanating from him, Morgan knew he'd spent the evening in his art studio. He spent most of his time there, immersed in the casts and sculptures that seemed dearer to him than his own children.

Morgan was probably the only one who cared about inattentiveness. Maggie had been fifteen when their mother died. She'd grown up quickly, stepping in to help raise Morgan and their younger brother, Ben, who was fourteen now and taller than Morgan. Ben had always been easy—'the Buddha baby,' Dad had called him. As long as he had snacks and video games, that boy was happy. Grammy had helped with all of them, but Maggie had always been the apple of Vivian Spencer's eye. Morgan's sister was smart and driven, polished and self-possessed in a way Morgan could never be.

Had never tried to be. She was the black sheep of the family, more so now that she was in high school and her inclination toward rebellion had found an outlet with the fast kids at her high school. She tended to fade into the background in the face of Maggie's perfection and Ben's affable nature. So when she'd discovered that she could get attention from the popular kids at school just by doing stupid things like playing chicken on the train tracks or toilet papering the principal's house, it had been fun. It made her feel like she belonged for the first time in her life. Who wouldn't want to belong?

But apparently she couldn't ignore her father when he decided to come out of his studio and play at being a responsible parent.

"I know," she relented with a shrug. "I'm sorry, Daddy. I'm trying."

"You are," he agreed, and she knew he meant it.

Guilt washed over her in response.

She hadn't meant to damage the building out at Harvest Vineyards. She'd been over the moon for a stupid boy, earning herself months of grounding and a one-way ticket to working the whole summer to pay for repairs to the tasting room building. She'd also lost her chance with Cole Maren, not that she'd ever really had him.

A boy like Cole wouldn't have time for a girl like her.

"Want a piece of marionberry pie before bed?" her dad asked. "Your grandmother brought one over earlier."

Morgan's stomach rumbled. Grammy's pie was her favorite. "Do we have ice cream?"

"Vanilla bean," he confirmed with his lopsided smile.

"Yum."

Maggie came home while Morgan was slicing the pie. Her sister joined them for a late-night snack, dutifully reporting on what they'd missed at Fall Fest, which wasn't much in Morgan's opinion.

Of course, she didn't ask if Cole had been there. He spent almost all his free time working at Harvest, so Morgan suspected he was behind the scenes at the winery's expansive booth. She'd seen little of him over the summer. He'd been avoiding her and now that they were back in school, he pretty much ignored her completely. It was awful.

"Are you okay?" she asked Maggie as they washed the plates after eating.

"Sure," Maggie said. "Just tired."

"Oh." Morgan studied her nearly perfect sister

from the corner of her eye. Maggie had haphazardly wiped away the butterfly painted on her cheek, and her eyes were red-rimmed, her hair mussed like she'd been running anxious fingers through it. "Was Griffin at Fall Fest?"

Maggie stilled, then flipped off the faucet. "He was there with a woman. A date, I think."

"I'm sorry." One more thing for Morgan to feel guilty about. Her sister's relationship with Griffin had gone off the rails after the fire. Apparently Griffin had said some unkind things about Morgan, most of them probably true. But Maggie was loyal, so they'd fought and that was the end of it.

"Me, too," Maggie whispered.

"Fries before guys," Morgan teased, hoping to make her sister smile. Needing Maggie to smile.

She did, and Morgan breathed a sigh of relief.

"I'm heading to bed." Maggie draped the towel she'd been using to dry the dishes over the handle of the stove. Dad had gone to the family room as soon as he'd finished his pie. He'd watch *The Tonight Show*, Morgan knew, and fall asleep in the tattered recliner he loved.

"Good night." She hugged Maggie.

"Foods before dudes," Maggie told her.

Morgan groaned. "So bad, Mags."

"'Night, Mo-Mo."

Morgan went up to her room and pulled the phone from her desk drawer. She was supposed to be grounded from it, too, but she'd placed her case upside down on the shelf in Dad's bedroom and he hadn't noticed the phone wasn't in it.

She responded to the flurry of text messages she'd

received during her family bonding time, then tucked a pillow under her covers in the shape of a sleeping body and opened the window to her second-story bedroom. A huge maple tree grew just in front of it. Trying to keep her heartbeat steady, she reached for a branch, swung onto it, then shimmied down the trunk.

A car was waiting at the end of the driveway, headlights turned off. With one look over her shoulder at her darkened house, she ran toward it through the shadows, pretending the guilt that flared inside her was excitement instead.

Chapter Three

Monday morning, Maggie turned her car up the winding drive that led to Harvest Vineyards for the first time since she and her father had brought Morgan to the Stone family home after the fire.

With less than two weeks until the hospital fundraiser, she couldn't avoid it any longer. She'd managed to hold the gala committee meetings at the hospital or at her office in town. Jana Stone, Griffin's mother, had attended all of them. She either hadn't noticed—or was polite enough not to comment—on Maggie's reluctance to make an appearance at the winery.

Today they were meeting to discuss decorations and a seating chart, so it couldn't be avoided any longer. Although that was exactly what Maggie wanted to do after her run-in with Griffin at Fall Fest. She felt branded by the unexpected kiss, all of the emotions she'd locked up tightly now spilling forth, like a dam had broken inside her.

The vineyard seemed almost fallow now that harvest season was over. As she drove closer to the heart of the operations, she could see the rows of vines spread out along acres of land, the leaves turning colors of burnished orange and yellow with the change of seasons.

In contrast to the serenity of the fields, activity bustled outside the new tasting room. Several cars and trucks were parked in front of the building, although Maggie didn't see Griffin's Land Cruiser. That wasn't a guarantee of his absence, so why did disappointment spear through her for a quick moment? It would be easier if she didn't see him today, she reminded herself. She didn't *want* to see him after the kiss. Better for both of them.

The building had a rustic farmhouse exterior with a stone veneer covering the bottom half. There were two chimneys and rough-hewn trusses that spanned the length of the building. A covered patio area took advantage of the expansive views of the vineyard below, and she could imagine tourists and locals alike enjoying long summer evenings around the built-in fire pit. The space was incredible and would definitely attract new visitors to the winery.

She took a deep breath as she exited her Volkswagen. The earthy scent of decaying leaves filled the air and although the vineyard was only twenty minutes from downtown, it felt like a world away. Had the property seemed this magical when it had been a regular farm, before Griffin's late father, Dave, had planted the first grapes that would transform the land and his family's fortunes?

"Hey, Maggie."

She turned to see her former fiancé moving toward her. It had only been four months since her runaway-bride move at the local church, where half the town had been waiting to see the powerful Spencer and Stone families united, but to her it felt like ages since she'd been with Trevor.

Well, ages wasn't too far off since the bedroom had never played a big role in their relationship. Theirs had been a union of convenience and practicality. Despite what he'd done to her and the price her reputation had paid for not revealing his betrayal, no emotion pinged through Maggie at the sight of him. Unlike with Griffin.

Trevor was safe, which was part of the reason she'd been with him in the first place.

"Hi, Trevor." She smiled and allowed him to give her a quick hug. "The building looks great."

He inclined his head. "I hate to give Griffin any credit, but he did a decent job." Trevor was a couple inches shorter than his brother and considerably leaner, with neatly trimmed hair and the kind of expensively tailored clothes that would have been more appropriate for the big city. Maggie had never quite understood what had made him return to his family's winery after college, although he was quite talented at his job as vice president of marketing for the vineyard.

In the five years since Trevor had taken over, Harvest had gone from a well-respected but relatively unknown winery to a national darling with several national and international award-winning vintages. Of course, a big part of the success was the quality of the wine, but Trevor's efforts at marketing and branding played a part, as well.

"It's more than decent," Maggie said gently. She understood the animosity that had simmered for years between the brothers: Griffin, the elder rebel, and Trevor, the golden boy and apple of his father's eye. But even though Griffin had hurt her with his rejection, she couldn't let Trevor discount what he'd done here. "It's incredible, Trev, and we both know it, especially given the setbacks he had because of—"

She broke off as Cole Maren, the former object of her sister's affection, walked out of the front of the tasting room, carrying a rolled-up set of plans under one arm. He glanced over and his steps faltered for a second as he met Maggie's gaze. His mouth curved into a ghost of a smile in greeting before he headed around the side of building.

"Yeah, incredible," Trevor admitted reluctantly. "Although I can't believe he kept that degenerate kid working here after his part in the fire."

"The fire was Morgan's fault," Maggie said clearly, "and she still feels terrible."

Trevor's eyes narrowed. "I still think she's covering for him."

"You know that's not—"

He held up a hand. "I don't want to argue with you. I know how you are when you believe in something." His mouth quirked. "A bulldog in a St. John's suit."

"It's Calvin Klein," Maggie corrected, color flooding her cheeks. In truth, she was as overdressed as Trevor for this meeting but she'd worn the chic fitted jacket and pencil skirt like a warrior might have donned his armor in medieval times. The suit made her feel braver than she knew herself to be. "Anyway, I appreciate how much your mom has done for the gala this year."

"She's enjoyed it." Trevor rocked back on his heels. "It gives her a purpose other than trying to come up with bonding experiences for Griffin and me."

"You're both dedicated to the vineyard. Isn't that something to bond over?"

"He walked away from us a decade ago." Bitterness laced Trevor's tone. "Had his own life in the army and working in construction until he deigned to once more grace us with his presence. That's not dedication. It's convenience and guilt over leaving in the first place. We'll see how long he lasts once his debt is paid."

By *debt*, Maggie knew Trevor was talking about the fire that had damaged the original tasting room, accidentally set by a teenage Griffin and several of his friends while they were partying. The careless mistake had led to a huge fight between Griffin and his dad, resulting in a rift among the Stone family that still hadn't been fully repaired.

"We'll agree to disagree," she said simply, unwilling to engage in this argument.

Trevor studied her for a long moment. "He's not here today, if you're wondering."

"I wasn't," she lied.

"He went to Seattle with his ex-girlfriend."

Maggie couldn't help but notice the note of triumph in Trevor's tone and kept her features placid. "We weren't expecting him at this meeting anyway. Is your mom around?" She glanced at the driveway. "The rest of the committee should be here shortly."

Trevor nodded. "She's finishing up a call. That's

actually why I'm here. She sent me over to tell you she'll be a few minutes late."

"No problem."

An awkward silence descended between the two of them.

"You don't have to wait with me," she told him after a moment.

His mouth tightened. "I miss our friendship."

"We're friends." She shrugged. "Just not the same kind as before."

"Want to grab a beer after work one night?"

"I…" She paused, unsure of how to answer. "Things are crazy with preparations for the gala." His mouth pulled down into a frown and she saw him sigh. "But after it's over, I'll have more time. Maybe then?"

"Great." Trevor flashed the boyish smile that was his trademark. "It's a plan."

He strode away from her and Maggie blew out a breath. Most of the time she loved living in a small town. She liked the familiarity of knowing her neighbors and the comfort that came from her routine. But some moments made her wish for the anonymity of big-city life. Like breaking up with someone and not having to worry about running into them or their mom or their brother or a dozen other mutual friends.

Her phone pinged and she pulled it from her purse. Her grandmother texting instructions on the size and placement of the centerpieces. She regretted encouraging Ben to teach Grammy how to text. It had quickly become her favorite means of lecturing Maggie.

"Ms. Spencer?"

She looked up to find Cole standing in front of her, looking like he hoped the ground would swallow him whole.

"Hey, Cole. I hear you've been a big part of keeping the tasting room renovations on track. Things look great."

"Thanks," he muttered, his gaze darting to hers before dropping again. The kid had probably grown three inches since Maggie had last seen him. He wore jeans and a Harvest Vineyards T-shirt with a small hole in the arm that looked like it came from catching it on a nail or something.

"I wanted to talk to you." His brow furrowed. "Duh. Obviously."

"What did you need?" She smiled, feeling sorry for the teen and his level of discomfort.

"It's Morgan." He looked at her, then away.

Maggie's smile froze. "What about her?"

"You need to— Your dad needs to watch her better. She's still running with the bad crowd."

"Your crowd?" she asked.

He gave a sharp shake of his head. "I'm steering clear of them, and Morgan should, too. They're not her real friends."

Maggie shrugged. "I appreciate your concern, Cole, and I'll talk to her. But we can't control who she's friends with at school. I wish—"

"What about on the weekends?"

"She's still grounded," Maggie said with a frown.

Cole took his phone from his back pocket and keyed in a code to unlock the home screen. He punched the screen again and then held up the phone to show Maggie a photo from one of the popular

social media sites. Morgan had her arm around another girl, both of them wearing too much makeup
and holding up red plastic cups.

The picture had been tagged "Saturday night she-
nanigans."

"When was this taken?" she demanded.

"Two nights ago."

After they'd had pie together and she'd gone to
bed.

"Why are you showing it to me?"

He shoved the phone back into his pocket. "I'm
telling you that group she's trying so hard to be a part
of is bad news. Trust me, Ms. Spencer."

"I do," she murmured and Cole's gaze returned to
hers, something like gratitude flashing in his eyes.
Maggie knew her sister had a wild streak, but she'd
thought the fire had taught her a lesson. Apparently
not.

"Do you two…um… Are you friends anymore?"

He shook his head. "We never were."

"That's not what Morgan thought," Maggie told
him. "I don't mean romantically, although I know
she had those kinds of feelings for you until…" She
glanced at the tasting room and saw Cole squirm.

"She's too good for me," he said, his voice flat,
"just like she's too good for the rest of the dumba—"
he cleared his throat "—the idiots she calls her
friends."

"You're not an idiot," Maggie insisted, "and my
sister clearly could use some friends who really care
about her."

He closed his eyes, chewing on his bottom lip like

he couldn't find the words for what he wanted to say. "Yeah," he mumbled finally.

"Think about it," she told him.

"Her dad… Your dad wouldn't like that," he said suddenly.

"Our father wants what's best for Morgan. He'd get used to it."

Cole tilted his head to one side, digesting that information. "I need to get back to work," he told her as a car pulled up the driveway.

She nodded. "Thank you."

He turned and walked toward the building. Maggie pressed a hand to her stomach, feeling nauseous. She hated to think of her sister still rebelling. Morgan had been hit hard by their mother's death from ovarian cancer, somehow taking the loss to heart in a different way than Maggie or Ben. She had a lot in common with their father, actually. Dad had retreated into his art and Morgan had dealt with her grief first through acting out in little ways and now in a full-blown rebellion.

But Maggie wouldn't give up on her sister. Morgan had a huge heart and so much potential. The election, fights with Grammy and Maggie's own tattered heart weren't nearly as important as Morgan. Maggie would do anything to make sure her sister stayed safe. Anything.

"Everyone was impressed by your work here."

"Great," Griffin answered absently, nailing a strip of weathered shiplap to the wall behind the tasting room bar. Most of the big items had been checked off the list: updated lighting for the room, expanded bathrooms for customers and a newly vaulted ceiling lined with reclaimed barn wood. The bar he'd had custom built by a renowned furniture maker north of Portland was due to be delivered next week.

The rest he was handling himself, with help after school from Cole. He was good at the general contractor piece, managing all the different subs and phases of a project. But he enjoyed working with his hands most of all, the satisfaction of creating something from nothing.

"It's going to be a wonderful event," his mother continued. "We've sold close to two hundred tickets."

The hammer stilled and he turned around at that bit of news. "Really? That seems like a lot of people." His skin itched at the thought of all those bodies and the conversation he'd be expected to make. Trevor thrived on that sort of stuff. His brother could glad-hand a fish if he thought it would increase exposure for the vineyard. Griffin still preferred to work behind the scenes.

"All those people are going to raise a lot of money for the new pediatric wing at the hospital."

"Sick kids are a big draw," he muttered.

"Griffin Matthew Stone." Jana Stone could communicate more saying his full name out loud than most politicians did throughout an entire career of making stump speeches. The blatant disapproval in her tone felt familiar, if off-putting.

He ran a hand through his hair. "I'm sorry. It's a worthy cause. I know that. Today was rough."

"Cassie's doing okay?" his mother asked, her voice gentling.

"Yeah. I've never seen someone with such a great

attitude. If optimism could cure cancer, she'd be well tomorrow."

Jana frowned. "I thought her prognosis was good."

"There's no sure thing," he answered, "and I can't shake the feeling she isn't telling me the whole truth. The business about a friendly visit down here, then insisting I go back to Seattle with her for a day to meet her son? It was strange."

"People have different ways of dealing with that kind of news. You did a good thing by making time for her."

"The boy is cute…" He picked up another board from the stack piled near the wall. "If you're into kids."

"Which you aren't," his mother said with an over-dramatic sigh.

"There's time for that."

"Maggie was here yesterday," Jana said casually.

He straightened and pointed the hammer at his mom. "That was the worst transition in the history of the world."

She shrugged. "Subtlety isn't my thing."

"No doubt."

"Sass," she said, lifting one brow.

"How is she?" He went back to measuring his next board as he asked the question, knowing if his mom saw his face she'd be able to read exactly what he was thinking. She'd always had that ability. It was damn annoying.

"Efficient and capable as ever. It's thanks to the changes she made to the event registration that helped us increase ticket sales so much. There's an app for RSVPs and it even tracks the silent auction items. People are already bidding and the gala isn't for two weeks. That girl really knows her stuff."

"Since when did you become such a Spencer fan?" he asked, biting down on the edge of a nail while he lifted the shiplap into place.

"I'm a fan of Maggie," his mother corrected.

He began hammering the wood, not wanting to continue this conversation. At all.

"So is Dr. Starber," she said loudly.

Griffin cursed as the hammer slammed against his thumb. He squeezed his fingers around the throbbing digit, bending forward and trying hard not to spit out the vilest words he knew. And that was saying something thanks to his years in the army and on various construction sites around the Pacific Northwest.

His mother tutted. "You should be careful. I can grab an ice pack from the main house."

He shook out his hand. "It's fine. Who's Dr. Starber?"

"He's the chief of pediatrics at Willamette Central Hospital," she reported. "He's a member of the planning committee and drops in on some of our meetings. We wanted his input on seating hospital staff."

Griffin snorted. "What kind of doctor has time to go to gala meetings?"

"The kind," Jana said with an eye roll, "who is interested in dating our Maggie."

Your Maggie. Our Maggie.

A muscle ticked in Griffin's jaw. In truth, he'd always thought of Maggie Spencer as her own person.

"What's this Dr. Feel Good look like?" he demanded.

"Tall, with sandy-blond hair, ruddy cheeks and blue eyes."

The man he'd seen talking to Maggie at the festival.

"He's not nearly as handsome as you." His mother patted his arm.

"I wasn't aware I was competing with him."

"Aren't you?"

"Mom, you know there's nothing going on with Maggie and me."

"There was not so long ago," she countered.

"It got complicated." The word tasted like ash in his mouth. He hated that word. *Complicated.*

"It's a relationship with a woman, Griffin." Jana sniffed delicately. "Of course things got complicated. She isn't a blow-up doll."

"Mom." He groaned. "Geez."

She waved off his embarrassment. "All I'm saying is that you'd better do something if you don't want to lose her."

"She isn't mine to lose."

"She should be."

He opened his mouth to argue but couldn't find the words. "Why are you pushing this?" he asked instead. "You don't even like the Spencers."

"That's not true." Jana crossed her arms over her chest. "Vivian Spencer is a bully and always has been. I don't care for her, but the rest of the family… They're good people."

"Even Morgan?"

"Those who live in glass houses…" his mom said gently and shame winged through Griffin. He'd been the king of adolescent stupidity in his time. "Morgan is a careless teenager who made a careless mistake. I don't think it means she's a terrible person. Maggie…

Well, I'll admit I was upset with how things ended between her and your brother."

Griffin dropped the hammer to one of the sawhorses and tapped a finger on his chin, as if contemplating her words. "I'm fairly certain you had visions of tackling her to the ground and clawing out her eyes."

"Always with the sass." She shook her head. "I see now that the match never would have worked. Trevor…" She paused. "Your brother has done an amazing job with the Harvest brand. But he has bigger dreams than Stonecreek. I don't want this life to limit him."

"He made the choice to come back after college," Griffin pointed out. "Dad made him the heir apparent. Trevor loves that."

"Trevor feels loyal because of that," she corrected. "It isn't the same thing. The vines aren't in his blood."

Griffin frowned as he thought about that. He'd never considered what it meant that his brother didn't feel the same way about the vineyard as he did. He was too busy being angry that Dad had chosen Trevor as his favorite and all but told Griffin he wasn't worthy to be a part of the family legacy.

"Anyway," his mom continued, "you've done an amazing job here and—"

"Was Dad my real father?" he blurted.

Jana's face paled and her eyes widened. "What would make you ask such a thing?" she asked in a choked whisper.

He wanted to close his eyes against the pain he saw in her gaze but forced himself not to look away.

He favored his mother's family in looks, the green eyes and olive-toned skin, whereas Trevor was the spitting image of their father. Griffin hadn't thought much about it as a kid, but as he'd grown older and his relationship with Dave Stone had deteriorated, he'd begun to question why his dad had seemed so unwilling to love him.

"He never liked me," he said and his mother's eyes filled with tears. "I just thought…if there was an explanation like—"

"You were his son," she said flatly. "His biological son."

"Huh." Disappointment and relief flooded Griffin in equal measure.

"Oh, Griffin." His mom moved forward, coming around the sawhorses to wrap her arms around him. "I've made my share of mistakes in life, and it kills me that you paid the price."

"What mistakes?" He pulled back to look at her. "If there wasn't another man…"

Jana wiped at her cheeks and sniffed.

"Mom, don't cry."

"It's fine," she told him, taking a step away. "I'm fine. But there was another man. A boy, really. We were so young, and I was in love. My family had moved here the summer before my senior year so my dad could take a job as a field hand. We were struggling, and Dad tended to be a messy drunk when he got down about our situation. We weren't exactly good stock."

"That's not how I remember Pops," Griffin argued.

"He cleaned himself up," she said with a nod. "But back then, it was bad." She smiled at him. "It's why

I'm so proud of how you've taken Cole under your wing. I wish I'd had someone like you in my life."

"You had Dad."

Her smile turned wistful. "Yes, I suppose I did, but it cost both of us. I'd been in love with someone else when I first met your father. The relationship didn't work out."

She looked so sad as she spoke the words. Outrage flared in Griffin at the thought that someone had hurt his mother. "Why?"

"It was complicated," she said, laughing softly. "I started dating your dad right after we broke up. Things progressed quickly." She shook her head. "I was on the rebound and we both knew it. He didn't care because we were having fun. Then I got pregnant."

"Did Dad think I wasn't his?" Griffin asked, his mouth dry.

"No, but I'm not sure we would have lasted without a reason to get married. Your father and Trevor had a lot in common. He had big dreams. Staying in Stonecreek wasn't part of his master plan, but with a wife and a baby... I didn't leave him with a lot of options."

"He shouldn't have blamed you," Griffin argued. "I'm sure you didn't mean to get pregnant."

Her gaze, which had always been the steadiest thing in his world, faltered. "I wanted a baby," she whispered. "I wanted something that belonged to me. Someone who couldn't leave me. Like I said, I was young and selfish, not thinking beyond what would make me happy." She looked up, her eyes bright with another round of tears. "You made me so happy."

"Dad didn't feel the same way."

Her mouth tightened into a thin line. "It all worked out. He inherited the farm and planted the vines. Actually, he had you and me to thank for that."

"How do you figure?"

"Your dad had saved enough money when I met him to go backpacking through Europe before he started college in the fall. He dropped out of school to get a job when I got pregnant and used the money for a down payment on the first house we bought. But when his dad died, we sold that house and moved here. I insisted he take the money and go to Europe. He came up with the idea for converting the farm to a vineyard in Italy."

Griffin laughed without humor. "Did he ever thank you for that? Because I don't remember his gratitude."

"It was there." Jana sighed. "He loved you in his own way."

"Just not the same way he loved Trevor," Griffin said, embarrassed that even as a grown man he still felt the lack of it.

"He'd be proud of who you've become."

"Thanks, Mom," Griffin said, although he wasn't convinced. At least he understood where his dad's animosity had come from, although the reason behind it was bogus.

She hugged him again. "Maybe you should ask Maggie to the gala."

"I wasn't planning on—"

"Don't finish that sentence," she said, squeezing his arms as she narrowed her eyes at him. "You're going. You'll wear a tux. You'll dance and make nice with people. And you'll like it."

"I won't like it."

"Fine. You don't have to like it, but it would mean a lot to me if you attended."

"Fine," he agreed. "I'm glad you're having fun with this, Mom. It suits you."

"It does." She winked. "Back to work now. We're close, but the tasting room has to be perfect."

"It will be."

"I know," she said as she walked away, glancing over her shoulder at him. "I trust you."

The words made his heart lighten. Despite everything they'd been through—all the complications life had thrown at them—his mother had always believed in him. Maybe she had a point and he shouldn't worry so much about complicated. There was the distinct possibility things were only as complicated as he made them to be in his mind.

One thing was simple to understand.

He hadn't stopped wanting Maggie. It might be time to focus on that once again.

Chapter Four

"How could you do it?" Morgan demanded, slamming her hand against Cole's open locker. The metal banged shut and he pulled off his wireless headphones to stare at her.

"I didn't do anything," he said flatly.

"You ratted me out to my sister." She'd been trying to track down Cole since Maggie and their dad had laid into her on Monday night, but she knew he wouldn't respond to her texts and he hadn't been at school yesterday.

He shrugged. "I talked to her. It's not a crime."

Even though a full day had passed, she was as angry as she'd been when first confronted about sneaking out. "I was already grounded. Now I have to go to her stupid office after school."

His gray eyes flashed with anger. "You might have been grounded, but that didn't mean you were staying home."

"How would you know?" she demanded. "You've dumped all your friends this year."

"They're not my friends." He stepped closer,

looming over her like he was trying to be intimidating. "They aren't yours, either."

"My life," she snapped, "is none of your business. You made it very clear you have no interest in me."

"I never said that," he whispered and unexpectedly reached out a finger to trace the seam of her ruby-red lips. "You're prettier without all the war paint."

She glared at him. "It's makeup," she said through clenched teeth. "Way to insult me."

One side of his mouth pulled up in the closest thing to a smile she'd seen on his face in months. "I meant it as a compliment."

"Oh." Morgan dabbed at the corners of her eyes, embarrassed and angry that tears pricked the backs of them. She glanced down at her fingertips, which came away black from the heavy eyeliner she'd taken to wearing because it bothered her grandmother so much.

"I was trying to do you a favor by talking to your sister," Cole said, his tone low and rumbly. Unlike a lot of boys in her class, his voice had changed completely, deepening so that he sounded like a man. He acted more mature than most guys she knew, too, even though the trouble he'd caused with his teenage antics before moving to Stonecreek was still plastered all over social media.

He'd told her—told everyone—that he'd changed. Maybe it was true. No one really saw him other than when he was at school. Morgan knew his home life was awful and he spent most of his free time out at Harvest Vineyards, working for Griffin.

"I got in more trouble," she said, jutting out her

chin. She wasn't quite willing to forgive him so easily.

"Not as much trouble as you're going to find if you don't drop the losers."

She gritted her teeth, unable to muster a decent comeback. The friends she hung out with now were the school's wild kids, more interested in ditching class and smoking pot under the bleachers than any kind of learning. Morgan didn't do drugs. She hadn't yet anyway, and although she always accepted a cup of whatever drink they were passing around, she mostly pretended to down it.

"I'm in with them now," she whispered. She'd worked so hard to rebel. The thought almost made her laugh. What kind of poser had to make a concerted effort to do the wrong thing? But it was easier to embrace the role of family miscreant. Compared to perfect Maggie and easygoing Ben, she was the oddball out. At least that was how she felt after her mom died eleven years ago.

Her throat stung as she grasped for memories of her kind, gentle mother. Mom had always loved Morgan just the way she was. Unlike Grammy. And who knew who Dad wanted her to be? He was so preoccupied with his studio that it was a wonder he even remembered her name.

She'd tried to follow in Maggie's footsteps—but the straight and narrow had never been a great fit for Morgan. She hadn't felt like she belonged anywhere until she'd started running with the wild kids last year. Ripped clothes, a constant sneer and the right kind of makeup, and she was set.

"You're not one of them," Cole told her. His eyes

crinkled at the corners and Morgan's heart gave a little thud. "You're better than that, Mo-Mo." She glared and he held up his hands, chuckling. "Sorry. I heard your dad call you that. It's cute."

"It's a name for a little girl," she muttered. "He doesn't want me to grow up."

"You're lucky he cares what you do."

Cole's voice was hollow, and shame filled her. He had moved to Stonecreek when his mom had taken off for parts unknown. She knew his dad was a raging alcoholic and his older brother had done jail time.

Morgan had lost her mom to cancer when she was only five years old. It was terrible, but she still had a family who loved her—even Grammy in her overbearing, judgmental way.

"I know," she whispered, then someone called her name. It was Jocelyn, her so-called best friend and the one who'd posted the photo online even though Morgan had asked her not to. "I've got to go," she said. Cole's gaze had gone blank again, a slight sneer curving his mouth.

"You don't have to." His lips barely moved, the words a whisper of breath, but she felt his anger like a slap in the face.

Her stomach tightened.

"Morgan, come on!" The call was insistent now.

"See you around," she said to Cole and whirled around to hurry toward her friend through the crowded hall, hating herself more with every step.

Friday night, Maggie walked into Over Cheesy, Stonecreek's popular pizza joint, at seven on the nose, then hesitated and almost backed out again.

She'd been compulsively punctual since childhood, always the first one in line outside the classroom each morning. Now she worried she was sending the wrong impression for a first date.

Too eager? No other plans?

It was bad enough that she had to meet her date at the restaurant, embarrassed to have him pick her up at her dad's house. Twenty-seven years old and living in her childhood bedroom. In all fairness, she'd sublet her house—Grammy's old house—because she'd planned to move into Trevor's place after the wedding. So eight months from now she'd be on her own again. That moment couldn't come too soon.

"Hey, Maggie, whatcha doin'?"

She forced a smile as she met the curious gaze of Britney Parker, a woman Maggie had known since kindergarten. Britney fluffed her already puffy blond hair and adjusted the formfitting black shirt she wore as part of her hostess uniform. Adjusted by tugging it down an extra inch.

"I'm…um…meeting a friend here," Maggie said, moving forward.

"Brenna?"

"No, actually—"

"Your grandma?"

Maggie flinched. Yikes. Was she so boring that people in town considered her friends with her grandma? She loved Grammy, but the nearly half-century age gap and the fact that most of their conversations ended in a lecture weren't conducive to much girl bonding.

"I have a date," Maggie offered before Britney could suggest their second-grade teacher as a potential companion. Then she glanced around to make sure no one had heard her. Of course, now that she'd outed herself to Britney, it would be no secret. Few secrets were kept in Stonecreek. As soon as she and James were seated at a table for two, the gossip train would chug right out of the station.

She glanced at her watch. Three minutes past seven. No need to panic. He probably had trouble finding a parking space, although there had been several near her car. Or he was just running late. He'd been the one to ask for her number, after all. Plus he'd actually called to set up their date. That was a good sign.

"Griffin," Britney said, her smile brightening.

"No," Maggie corrected. "He's—"

"Hey, Brit."

Maggie stiffened at the sound of the familiar voice behind her. Then he was at her side, heat radiating from his big body. She caught the scent of cloves and mint gum and her traitorous knees went a little weak.

"You two giving it another try?" Britney's gaze swung between Maggie and Griffin.

She glanced at him, shocked to see one thick brow cock in what looked like... Was that hope on his face?

"We're not," she said quickly. "I'm meeting someone else."

"Then I don't think he's here yet," Britney said. "I'll get a table set up, though. What about you, Griffin?"

He scrubbed a hand over his face. "Trevor and I are grabbing dinner."

"Here?" Maggie squeaked.

Britney stifled a laugh. "Awk-ward."

"It's probably a sign," Griffin said, none too helpfully as far as Maggie was concerned.

"It's not a sign," she told him.

"Are you kidding?" Britney picked up her phone
and started thumbing the screen. "It's bad enough
that you started dating your ex-fiancé's brother. Now
the two of them have to watch you on a first date?"
She glanced up. "It's a first date, right?"

"Yes."

Maggie whirled around to find Dr. James Starber
standing behind her. She'd been so distracted by Griffin and the mortification of this situation that she hadn't
even noticed him enter the restaurant.

"You're on a date, Mags?"

Maggie thunked the heel of her palm against her
forehead as Trevor appeared directly behind James,
who looked back and forth between the two Stone
brothers like he was afraid he'd stumbled into the
middle of a kinky small-town threesome or something.

"I'm trying," she told Trevor with a tight smile,
then turned back to Britney. "Could we get a table?
Now."

"Sure thing." The blonde grinned, then held up
her phone. Maggie blinked as the flash went off. "I
just need photographic evidence of this moment. I
won't tag you if that makes it easier."

Maggie inwardly cringed. "*Please* don't tag me."
She looked over her shoulder and gave James what she
hoped was an encouraging smile. "Nice to see you."

"Um…" He massaged the back of his neck. "You,
too."

"Take care of this one," Trevor said with a hearty back slap to James. "She's something special." He wagged a finger between himself and Griffin, clearly relishing how uncomfortable this was making both Maggie and his brother. "We can vouch for that."

"Shut up, Trevor," Maggie and Griffin said at the same time.

"Right this way," Britney announced cheerily, and without looking at Griffin again, Maggie followed the other woman.

She slid into the seat, ignoring the curious gazes of the diners at the tables around them. "I'm sorry about that," she said to James when they were alone. Or as alone as they could be with half the restaurant staring at them.

He flashed a half-hearted grin. "I'm from Chicago and did my residency in Boston," he told her. "This is my first stint at small-town living. I think I got a crash course on what exactly that means tonight."

"Yeah," she agreed. "It's actually great most of the time."

"I remember hearing talk at the hospital about a runaway bride. It seemed like a big scandal."

Maggie grimaced. "Unfortunately they were talking about me. Long, boring story."

The waiter came at that moment and took their drink orders. James debated which pinot noir was the best choice from the selections offered, and without hesitation Maggie steered him toward one from Harvest. It was the same one she and Griffin had shared their first night together. Even when she got away from Griffin Stone, she couldn't seem to escape his hold on her.

She didn't notice Griffin and Trevor being seated, so either they'd chosen a table behind her or, hopefully, picked another restaurant. She couldn't help but be curious as to why they were having dinner together. Normally the brothers barely got through a casual conversation without arguing.

James was nice and interesting, obviously dedicated to his patients, but Maggie felt not an iota of a spark between them. Not even the potential for one, although when she tilted her head and squinted slightly, James bore an uncanny resemblance to a young Robert Redford. She was truly off her game if she couldn't manage a spark for a Redford look-alike. Then he explained his plan to move back to Chicago once his fellowship at Willamette Central was finished. She listened as he extolled the highlights of the Windy City, but had to admit she had no interest in discovering for herself what Chicago had to offer.

Overall the meal was pleasant and the pizza fantastic as always. James walked her to her car, the streets empty as Stonecreek tended to roll up the sidewalks early, even on weekend nights.

"Thank you for a lovely evening," she said, pasting a bright smile on her face as she pulled her keys from her purse. She hoped he wouldn't try to kiss her because that would make the next two weeks working on the hospital fund-raiser far too awkward.

His mouth quirked. "As first dates go, that was a total dud, right? You're not into me at all."

"Um…" She felt color rise to her cheeks. "You seem like such a nice guy."

"Kiss of death," he murmured.

"No," she argued. "But I'm not… Things are… It's complicated." *Ugh, that word again.*

"I get it," he told her.

She laughed softly. "Then maybe you can explain it to me."

"There was this girl I dated when I was an under-graduate," he said almost wistfully. "We met senior year. I was applying for med school and she was an elementary education major. She was beautiful and funny. When we were together I forgot all about the stress and pressure of everything else."

"I love when that happens." Maggie thought of the one blissful night she'd spent with Griffin and how everything but the two of them had faded into the background.

"She wanted to make things more serious, but I was consumed with my future. It didn't seem like a relationship had any place in it." His brow creased. "Things were too complicated."

"I'm sorry," Maggie whispered.

He shook his head. "Me, too. I should have never let her go. Now I can see that none of the excuses I gave were worth a damn."

"Maybe it's not too late," she suggested. "Things are steadier for you now. I'm sure you could track her down on social media." Even though she didn't know James well, she liked him. What she didn't like was the pain she saw in his kind eyes.

"We're Facebook friends," he confessed, then sighed. "She's married with one little boy and an-other baby on the way. She looks happy."

"James."

He shrugged. "I'm happy for her. I am. But I can't

help but think it should be me in those pictures. I was so focused on my future and my goals. Now that I've achieved them, it doesn't seem to matter. Not one bit."

She leaned in and hugged him. "I'm sorry. There's someone else out there for you. I know it."

"Thanks," he said when she pulled away. "I'm not trying to be Donnie Downer, but when you said *complicated* it struck a nerve. Things can seem complicated but only when we let that take over. What really matters is usually pretty simple."

Maggie's breath caught. "You're right."

"Of course." He winked. "I'm a doctor. We're always right."

She laughed, which she knew had been his intention. Lightening the moment.

"I did have a really good time tonight."

He nodded. "I'll see you at the next gala meeting," he told her and walked toward his car.

Maggie got into hers, turning it on and cranking the heat against the chill of the October night air. The cold seemed to settle in her bones. She gripped the steering wheel, the conversation with James tumbling through her mind. Seeing Trevor and Griffin. The way Griffin had looked at her in the restaurant.

Finally she backed out, but as she turned the corner a block down, her gaze snagged on a familiar blue Land Cruiser parked at the curb in front of O'Malley's Tavern.

Without thinking, she pulled in behind Griffin's SUV.

The bar was crowded with locals and a few tourists. If someone wanted a late-night drink, O'Malley's was the place to be in Stonecreek.

"Hey, Ms. Mayor," Chuck O'Malley, the tavern's gregarious owner, called from behind the bar. "Is this an official campaign stop?"

Maggie waved at the people who turned to say hello, once again finding all eyes on her. Everyone turned except Griffin, seated at the end of the bar, his broad shoulders stiff as he gazed down into the glass of brown liquor in front of him.

"I'm off the clock tonight," she told Chuck, even though she was never truly off.

"Then what can I get you?" he asked.

"My usual," she told him, moving forward.

He rolled his eyes but grinned. "You got it."

She made small talk with a few of the patrons before climbing onto the bar stool next to Griffin. "This seat taken?"

He picked up his glass and took a long drink. "Looks that way."

"You and Trevor must have had a short dinner," she said, hanging her purse on the hook next to her stool. "I didn't see you in the restaurant again."

"We ended up at The Kitchen. Over Cheesy felt a little crowded."

"Sorry," she mumbled. "Although, Friday is fish taco night at The Kitchen, so that's a plus."

Griffin gave a small laugh. "Yeah, I guess."

"Here you go, Maggie." Chuck placed a glass in front of her. "I feel like I should warn you that Jason has been canvassing the downtown business owners, offering all kinds of campaign promises about how he's going to lower taxes and add incentives to the mix if we throw our support behind him."

Maggie's chest tightened. This was why she was

never really off the clock. "I figured as much," she said. "A few people around town have been fairly conspicuous about avoiding eye contact with me in the past couple of weeks. I appreciate you confirming it."

Chuck nodded. "Can he really make that happen?"

Maggie couldn't help but hear the hope in the man's voice. "Not exactly. Any new tax breaks would have to go through council. The mayor can't arbitrarily make that kind of decision. I'm sure that's why Jason hasn't spoken publicly about it. But it sure sounds promising."

"It does," Chuck said, running a hand through his thinning brown hair.

"There's a downtown business owners' meeting next week, right?" Maggie asked.

Chuck nodded.

"Let me push some of the council members to see where they stand on things. I've also got some ideas for a new marketing campaign that I'd like to run by all of you. It would keep people coming into town even through the winter season."

"You're a gem, Maggie." Chuck reached out and patted her hand. "I'll tell Frank to put you on the agenda. I know you have our best interests at heart."

One of the waitresses called to Chuck and he headed for the other end of the bar.

"Your drink is pink," Griffin said after several moments of awkward silence.

"Cranberry juice and club soda," Maggie confirmed.

"Living on the wild side."

"I had wine with dinner."

He glanced at her, cocking an eyebrow.

"A Harvest pinot noir. The 2015 vintage. Aroma of black cherries overlaid with fennel and a smoky finish."

"One of my favorites," he said, nodding.

"I know," she whispered.

"Your date seemed nice."

"He is." She paused, then added, "Also pining over an ex-girlfriend."

"Imagine that," Griffin murmured.

"She's married now. Things were too complicated when they were together, so he let her go. He regrets it."

He swiveled on his bar stool, ice clinking in the glass as he balanced it between two fingers. "You spent the date talking about how much he misses his ex-girlfriend?"

It sounded ridiculous and Maggie laughed softly. "Not all of it."

"What's on the agenda for the second date?" Griffin asked, draining his glass. "Dissecting dysfunctional family Christmases from when he was a kid?"

Maggie sipped at her drink. "We won't have a second date."

She saw his shoulders relax slightly.

"Does that make you happy?" she asked, narrowing her eyes at him.

"Delirious with it," he confirmed with a wink.

"Why?"

The question seemed to surprise him. A muscle ticked on the side of his jaw and he looked past her, raising his glass. She assumed he was looking at

Chuck and, as expected, the bar owner appeared a moment later.

"Another Jack?" he asked.

"Please."

Chuck turned to Maggie. "More of the mayor's special?"

She shook her head. "I'm heading out. Thanks again for the intel, Chuck."

"I've owned this place for twenty-five years," he told her. "I've never seen anyone work as hard for this town as you, Mayor Spencer. That counts for a lot in my book."

A tumble of emotions clogged her throat as she nodded and pushed away from the bar. It was all too much…too… No, she wouldn't use that dreaded word again. But between her family, the campaign and her heart, Maggie felt wrung out and hung up to dry with all her vulnerable bits exposed for everyone to see. She couldn't deal with any more tonight.

As Chuck walked away to refill Griffin's glass, Maggie grabbed her purse and turned.

A warm hand on her arm stopped her. She faced him again, searching his green gaze for a clue as to how he felt about her. His eyes gave nothing away.

"Why did you come in here tonight?" he asked, his voice a low rumble.

"I saw your car."

He arched a brow. "And…?"

"No," she said, shaking her head. "I've already told you how I felt…how I feel. It's your turn, Griffin. I'm getting whiplash from your mixed signals. You don't want me to date another man, but you don't want me for yourself."

"I…" He closed his eyes. "I don't know what to say."

"That's *your* issue." She tugged her arm away from his grasp. She wasn't sure what she'd expected from him tonight. The way he'd looked at her earlier in the restaurant had given her some ridiculous hope. But if he couldn't even admit he wanted her, it left them with nothing.

Once again she was left with nothing.

She deserved more.

He stared at her and the heat in his gaze made her tingle all the way to her toes. It wasn't enough.

"Hope your friend Jack makes you happy," she told him. "At least he won't expect too much." Then she walked away, her head held high. She wouldn't break down again. Not for Griffin Stone.

Chapter Five

"How was the meeting with Trevor?" Marcus Sanchez asked Griffin on Monday morning.

"Pointless," Griffin snarled, then blew out a breath when the other man raised a brow. He didn't deserve to be on the receiving end of Griffin's bad mood. Marcus had first come to work for Harvest Vineyards as a young man. He'd quickly showed a deep understanding of the grapes as well as a knack for dealing with the business side of things, and his expertise had made him an indispensable part of the operation as the winery grew. After Griffin's father's sudden death, Jana had named Marcus CEO in a move that surprised many, including Trevor, who Griffin knew had assumed himself the heir apparent.

"Sorry," he muttered. "My brother and I can barely agree on an appetizer to order. I'm not sure what made me think he'd want my opinion on our wholesale distribution channels."

Marcus glanced around the tasting room, which was flooded with morning light. "Construction is almost complete. We need to determine what your role in the company is going to be moving forward, so you and Trevor will have to find some common ground."

"I haven't committed to staying," Griffin said.

"Harvest needs you," Marcus answered simply.

"You've been talking to my mother." Griffin picked up the can of stain he was using to deepen the color on the wood planks that covered the back wall.

"No, although I imagine she's of the same opinion."

"Oh, yeah."

"You have an affinity for the vines, Griffin. It can't be denied."

"I have other jobs in the pipeline," Griffin countered, dipping a paintbrush into the stain. "In fact, one of the developers I work with in Seattle has a new project starting next month. He needs a general contractor."

Marcus slammed his hand on the hewed wood of the top of the bar. It was a massive outburst for Marcus, who was one of the most even-tempered men Griffin had ever met. "You're a winemaker, Griffin Stone."

"I never got that chance." Griffin concentrated on applying even rows of stain to the wood, focusing so that his hand didn't tremble. Marcus's words brought up long-buried emotions. "Dad kicked me out of here and we both know he had good reason for it."

Out of the corner of his eye Griffin saw Marcus smooth his hand over the bar, as if making amends for accosting it moments earlier. "We both know you're different now. Prove it."

Something inside Griffin came to life at the challenge. It had been his dream while spending his childhood exploring the neat rows of vines his father had planted. With every expansion of the vineyard, Griffin's mind had exploded with ideas and plans for the future. Until the animosity between him and his dad had poisoned his aspirations.

And there it was. The old anger, the fear and doubt that he wasn't worthy. That he'd mess things up, as he had so many times as a kid.

He'd tagged along during every stage of the growing season, soaking in all he could about the life cycle of the vines and how the grapes were affected by nature. He'd loved both the science and the art of it, but nothing he'd done had been good enough for his father. He couldn't handle the delicate fruit. He wasn't careful enough. He got in the way.

It had been different with Trevor, who back then could have cared less about the family business. But Dad had encouraged Trevor whenever he'd showed any interest, even with Griffin standing on the sidelines, chomping at the bit to be involved.

His father's favoritism had tainted Griffin, both toward his brother and Harvest Vineyards. He still couldn't understand the point of it. As his mother had said, Dave Stone had ended up with a good life, a successful business and the respect of his peers. But he'd never left Stonecreek, other than quick business trips. Maybe that was the point. Griffin's dad hadn't been able to choose his life, while Griffin had. He'd joined the army, seen the world, served his country and become his own man. Dad had returned to the farm he'd hated growing up, and spent his days working the land, something he'd never planned for or wanted.

All that history was another set of complications, just like the obstacles keeping him and Maggie apart.

But Griffin had a choice. He could let the past define him and allow his doubts to win, or he could choose a different way. A way forward.

"Trevor doesn't want me here any more than Dad did," he said, still not quite able to let go of the past.

"Make it work," Marcus said simply.

Griffin huffed out a laugh and dipped the paintbrush into the can of stain again. "Why does this conversation feel like some kind of vintner version of a Jedi mind trick?"

Marcus leaned forward on the bar. "You belong at Harvest."

"Your confidence means a lot," Griffin admitted, drawing in a breath. "Do you think it would help if I reminded Trevor that the reason I returned here in the first place was to attend his wedding?"

Marcus shook his head but his eyes danced with amusement. "Doubtful." He straightened. "That reminds me, I'm leaving early today to attend a pre-debate rally for Maggie."

"There's an actual debate?"

"Your cousin is insisting on it to rattle her. He doesn't play fair."

"It seems strange to think of political machinations in Stonecreek." He rubbed a hand across the back of his neck. "Is there a chance Maggie could lose the election?"

Marcus shrugged. "Unfortunately yes. According

to Brenna, she's working her butt off to make sure that doesn't happen."

"Good for her," Griffin murmured.

"She needs all the support she can get," Marcus said with a pointed look.

"I need to get back to staining. I'll think about what you said and try with Trevor again. That's all I can offer." Griffin dropped his gaze, wishing he had something more to give.

Maggie brushed an invisible speck of lint from her suit jacket that evening as she stood behind the curtain of the high school's packed auditorium.

"Standing room only out there," Brenna told her.

"Slow night in town," Maggie answered with a forced laugh. It was still difficult to believe so many people cared about the mayor's race. The first time she'd been elected, after her grandmother had announced her impending retirement, Maggie had sponsored a few pancake breakfasts and met with most of the local businesses and civic organizations. Then she'd been elected, running unopposed, as if holding the office was her right.

She had no problem proving she deserved to be reelected but Jason's campaign felt weirdly personal, like he was more interested in taking her down than building himself up. Maybe it was a reflection of the state of politics on a national level, or the town's fascination with her personal life over the past few months, but Maggie didn't like it.

Marilee Haggard, the town council member who was moderating the debate, announced each of the candidates and gave a brief rundown of their respective résumés.

"You've got this," Brenna whispered, then Maggie walked out, smiling and shaking hands with Jason Stone as they met in the middle of the stage.

They took their places behind podiums that had been set up on either side of the stage, angled so that they faced both each other and the audience.

"I have to admit I'm relieved at the handshake," Jason said into the microphone, glancing between Maggie and the crowd. "I was a little afraid the mayor would expect me to bow, given that she's a Spencer and I'm just a peon member of the Stone family."

There was a smattering of laughter from the audience and Maggie felt color rise to her cheeks. "I'm not like that," she said, bending toward her microphone, "and I think everyone here knows it, Jason."

"Do they?" Jason threw up his hands in an overly dramatic gesture. Seriously, had the guy been involved in the theater department in high school? "Because you've made it clear by your actions that we're not good enough for you. Ask my cous—"

"Can we keep on point with election issues?" Maggie asked, hating the thread of annoyance she couldn't keep out of her voice. She didn't want people to see her as a shrew, but how many times did she have to defend her decision not to marry Trevor before this town let it go?

Marilee nodded. "Of course. The first issue we're going to tackle tonight involves funding for essential services and emergency management. Jason won the coin toss backstage, so he'll answer first."

As Maggie listened to Jason make his points, she scanned the audience to gauge the reaction to the patented lies he was spewing. Her opponent was good, she'd give him that much. He skirted the truth about how things were being handled currently and stayed vague on the changes he'd make to improve it.

Her dad, grandmother, Morgan and Ben were in the front row. Dad watched Jason with an unmistakable scowl, and Maggie wondered how much her father even understood the issues in town. So much of his life was spent consumed by his art, with occasional moments of parental involvement. He was getting better, she'd admit, and appreciated his efforts to stay connected with Morgan and Ben.

Grammy, on the other hand, shook her head and made little huffs of disapproval, her razor-sharp gaze snapping between Jason and Maggie. Maggie almost expected her to rush the stage and tackle Jason outright to shut him up. Morgan and Ben both looked bored out of their minds, which Maggie expected. Brenna and Marcus sat behind them and... She sucked in a sharp breath. Griffin occupied the chair next to Marcus.

How had she not seen him immediately? As if sensing her gaze, his attention shifted from his cousin to her and he flashed a quick half smile.

"Maggie?" She blinked and glanced at Marilee. "Did you want to respond to the question?" the woman asked.

"Um...yes... I—"

"Or is it beneath you to actually concern yourself with issues that matter to this town?" Jason asked, sarcasm dripping from his tone.

Maggie felt her temper flare as a disapproving murmur of voices filled the room.

"This town matters to me a great deal," she said directly to her opponent. "So much so that I returned here as soon as I graduated college to dedicate my time and energy to it."

Jason nodded. "Young and inexperienced. You admit it."

"Enough." She held up a hand. Yes, she'd been groomed to lead Stonecreek, but Maggie had never taken her place in the community for granted. "People here know me." She looked out to the audience and, while she didn't let her gaze drift to Griffin's, she saw him nodding as if encouraging her to finally stand up for herself. "I've focused on the arts as a growth factor for tourism, spearheaded the plans for a dedicated community center building and managed to hold property taxes at the current rate. Just this week I met with the owners of the local businesses to discuss a new marketing campaign to bring visitors here during winter months." She pointed a finger at Jason. "How long have you lived in Stonecreek?"

He stiffened and snorted out a disbelieving laugh. "I grew up here. You know that."

"But you left for college on the East Coast, correct?"

"So what?"

"You've been back a year now?" she demanded.

"I have vast experience in the world," he countered. "It adds to my plans for the town."

"About those plans," she said, wrinkling her nose. "You told everyone that you'd give a tax break to any business that's been established for at least five years. Actually, only the council has the power to vote on business tax laws. In my experience as mayor..." She paused, then added, "Emphasis on the word *experience* since I'm the only candidate who has experience in local government."

"That doesn't—"

She held up a hand. "Do *not* interrupt me. You had your time. This is mine. A campaign promise is only as good as your ability to follow through on it. I'm a proponent of feasible growth and realistic change..."

Jason crossed his arms over his chest. "You got the job because of your grandma and everyone knows it. There hasn't been someone strong enough to stand up to the Spencers until me."

"Being strong isn't the same as bullying people," Maggie said clearly into the microphone. "You've spent more time taking jabs at my character and personal life than understanding what makes this town work and what the residents need."

"Are we ready for the next question?" Marilee asked cheerfully.

"I understand that the mayor should have the best interests of all residents in mind," Jason said, ignoring the moderator's question. "Not just the people in her own social circles."

"I don't do that," Maggie said immediately.

"Every decision you make benefits your family and your grandmother's circle of cronies."

"That isn't true." Embarrassment washed through Maggie. She'd taken her grandmother's advice on so many aspects of the job. Only recently had she begun to question whether Grammy truly wanted to help Maggie do what was right for all facets of the town's population.

"As far as your personal life…" Jason continued. "In a place like Stonecreek, character counts for a lot. It seems to me—" he looked out to the audience "—as well as to a number of other people, that you were willing to marry into my family like some people enter into a business merger. What kind of moral compass does that exhibit?"

"Trevor and I care about each other but made the decision together that the marriage wouldn't work," Maggie said, hating that she was trotting out her dirty laundry for public consumption once again. "It had nothing to do with my position as mayor."

"Such a pat answer," Jason said. "But no one around here believes it, Maggie. Everything you do is planned and controlled, most of it by your ever-present grandmother."

"Don't bring Grammy into this," Maggie said on a hitch of breath.

Marilee stood. "I really must insist—"

"Then explain why it happened. How can we believe you won't—"

"He cheated on me," Maggie blurted and heard gasps of shock from the audience. She glanced at the front row to where her father looked furious, her grandmother incredulous. Morgan and Ben both stared at her with their mouths wide-open.

She couldn't bear to look at Griffin at that moment. Yes, he'd encouraged her to tell the truth, but she knew he hadn't meant in this kind of a public forum.

Trevor would be blindsided and Jana humiliated once again.

She wiped at her eyes and glared at Jason. "Are you happy now?" she asked into the microphone.

"I…" He shook his head. "I didn't know."

"Because it was none of your business," she told him, then turned to the audience. "It was no one's business. For the last time, I'm sorry all of you were so very disappointed that Trevor and I didn't marry. It was never my intention to let down the town. But things came to light just before the ceremony that made it impossible for me to go through with it."

Shame burned in her gut at having to relive the betrayal. She'd worn the mantle of Maggie Spencer, runaway bride, because it had seemed easier than being forever known as the cuckolded fiancée. Now she was going to get a taste of both.

She drew in a breath and addressed Marilee. "I'm afraid we've gotten quite off track this evening."

The other woman nodded, her mouth opening and closing like a fish flailing on a dock.

"I've also done all the talking I can stand for now," Maggie said quietly. "I apologize that we didn't make it through your questions. Email them to me and I'd be happy to offer my responses to be published so that everyone understands my position on things."

Without waiting for an answer, she turned and fled the auditorium.

Chapter Six

Griffin knocked on the door of Jim Spencer's house later that night, unsure of what he was doing there. Even less certain when Morgan opened it.

Her gaze dropped briefly when she saw him and pink stained her cheeks.

"Is Maggie here?" he asked.

"Morgan…" Jim's deep voice came from the hallway. "Tell whoever it is that—" He stopped when he saw Griffin and shook his head. "Not tonight. She's been through enough."

"That's why I'm here," Griffin said quickly, holding out his hand to prevent Maggie's sister from shutting the door in his face. "I want to make sure she's okay. I texted and called but—"

"She turned off her phone," Morgan reported. "About a million texts came in after the meeting. Someone posted a video on YouTube."

Griffin cursed under his breath.

"We had it taken down," Jim told him.

"She didn't do anything wrong," Griffin said, fisting his hands at his sides.

"We know that," her father answered.

"So does my family," Griffin offered, hitching his chin. "I talked to Trev and Mom after I left the high school. I didn't want them blindsided by what happened."

"You don't seem surprised at her revelation about Trevor and the wedding." Jim crossed his arms over his big chest. For a guy pushing middle age and who often had his shirt buttoned wrong, Jim Spencer looked surprisingly strong. And intimidating.

"Maggie told me a while ago."

"Did Jana know?" Jim demanded.

Griffin shook his head. "She had no idea. I wanted Trevor to tell her but…"

"What he put my daughter through was terrible," Jim said, his voice icy, "on many levels. First the betrayal—"

"On her wedding day," Morgan snarled, eyes narrowed at Griffin. "My sister didn't deserve that crap from him."

Jim put his hand on her shoulder. "Go tell her Griffin's here. Maggie will decide whether he comes in or not."

"I hope she says no," Morgan whispered, then turned and disappeared down the hall.

No, Griffin wanted to shout. *Don't let her shut me out.* He needed to see her. He needed to make her understand—

"You have to take some blame in this," Jim said.

Griffin took a step back like the older man had punched him. "What do you mean?" He shook his head. "I wasn't even here. I didn't know he was cheating. Hell, I gave him a black eye at the church after Maggie told me what he'd done."

Jim inclined his head, nodding as if he approved of that bit of retribution. "But after you found out, you still let her take the blame."

"That was Maggie's decision," Griffin argued even as guilt speared through him. He should have told someone, forced her or Trevor to reveal the truth of what had caused the breakup. He hated how people treated her because they thought she'd walked away from his brother.

"You still should have—"

"No."

They both turned as Maggie walked into the entry. She'd changed from the conservative suit she'd worn at the debate to a pair of black sweatpants and a University of Oregon T-shirt. Her face had been scrubbed of makeup, which only made her more beautiful to Griffin. Yet he couldn't stand the shadows under her eyes or the defeated slump of her shoulders.

"Griffin tried to convince me to tell people the truth. I know he pushed Trevor for the same thing." Her brow furrowed as she looked at her father, like she could will him to understand. "It was my choice and he respected it."

"I still don't understand," her dad said, throwing up his hands. "Trevor was a snake. You let him get away with it."

She winced and Griffin wanted to step between the two of them to shield Maggie from any more recrimination.

"Maybe," she admitted softly, "I was embarrassed. The choice was to be the runaway bride or the woman who couldn't keep her fiancé's attention, even on her wedding day. That option was too pathetic, Dad."

"You aren't pathetic," Jim said, enveloping her in a tight hug. "I have half a mind to drive out to the vineyard and kick Trevor's butt into next week."

"I think Mom's taking care of that," Griffin offered. "She was pretty mad."

Jim looked over his shoulder. "Your mother is a good woman."

"The best," Griffin agreed.

"Dad, I'm going to talk to Griffin for a few minutes," Maggie said, stepping away.

"You don't have to," her father told her. "You don't owe anyone with the last name Stone another minute of your time."

Griffin wanted to protest but Jim was right.

Maggie lifted a hand and pressed her palm to her dad's cheek. "Ben needs help with his science lab," she said gently.

"I'm useless at science," her dad said with an eye roll.

"He's coloring a cell diagram."

Jim perked up. "Coloring I'm good at. I'll get the oil pastels."

"That might be a little much for eighth-grade science."

"Then Ben should love it."

"Can I come in?" Griffin asked Maggie when they were finally alone.

She blinked as if she hadn't realized he was still standing on the front porch. "Of course. Sorry. Dad should have invited you in from the start."

"He was in full-stop protective mode." Griffin shut the front door behind him.

She smiled, clearly trying to make it bright, but Griffin could see a painful tightness compress the edges of her mouth. "Was that your first town meeting?" she asked.

He nodded.

"You picked a good one. Your cousin and I put on quite a performance."

"Don't do that," he whispered. "You don't need to play it off with me."

He reached for her but she shrugged away, shaking her head. "I don't know if I'm in a place where I can let you touch me."

His chest ached at the raw honesty of that admission. "I'm sorry my cousin is a goading jerk."

"I didn't mean to announce Trevor's cheating to the whole town." She ran a hand through her hair, tugging on the ends. "Did you talk to him?"

Griffin nodded.

"Is he mad?"

"Do you care?"

"I do."

The two words she would have said on her wedding day if his brother hadn't cheated. "Why?" he couldn't help but ask.

"I never wanted to hurt Trevor."

"After what he did to you..."

"Even so. I promised I'd keep his betrayal a secret, and I broke my word."

"Jason pushed you to it." Griffin moved past her, gripped the handrail of the staircase that led to the second floor. "I went to his house tonight, too. Big wimp wouldn't come to the door. All the lights went out while I was standing on the porch, like I was supposed to believe he suddenly wasn't at home."

"Do you blame him?" Maggie asked, and he heard a sad kind of amusement in her voice.

"I blame him for most of this," Griffin said, turning around to face her. "If he wants to run against you as mayor, have at it. But to try to win the election by assassinating your character is low. He always was a loser."

"I shouldn't have let him bait me."

"Stop doing that. Stop taking the blame when other people are awful. This wasn't your fault. Calling off the wedding wasn't your fault." He paused, then added softly, "The things that went wrong between us definitely weren't your fault."

"You never answered me about Trevor."

He sighed. "He's not mad at you. I imagine he's not loving the tongue lashing he's getting from Mom, but he seemed almost resolved to the truth being out there."

"I'll talk to him tomorrow."

"Talk to me right now."

Her head tilted as she studied at him. "Isn't that what we're doing?"

"You're standing a few feet from the front door," he reminded her. "I keep waiting for you to kick me out."

"I don't understand why you're here," she told him, which wasn't exactly an invitation to stay.

"I hate what happened to you tonight. I wanted to make sure you're okay."

"I'm okay," she whispered.

"Let me in, Maggie May," he coaxed. "I probably don't deserve another chance, but give me one anyway."

She closed her eyes and drew in a long breath, then blew it out. "I'm binge watching *Gilmore Girls* on Netflix," she told him when she opened her eyes again. "I needed a distraction."

He lifted an eyebrow. "I could Netflix and chill tonight."

She laughed, rolling her eyes. "How do you feel about Netflix and sitting on the couch with my dad in his bedroom down the hall?"

"That works, too." He would have agreed to anything to be near her tonight.

He followed her down the hall and into the cozy family room off the kitchen. Jim, Morgan and Ben were nowhere to be seen and Griffin wondered if Maggie's dad was purposely giving them time alone. If so, it was the most outright vote of confidence Griffin could have asked for given Jim's earlier attitude.

She lowered herself onto the couch, glancing up at him almost warily before patting the cushion next to her. "Are you sure about this? I'm not great company right now, and it isn't going to be sexy times. I can't even promise to be able to string together a decent sentence."

"Any sentence that includes the phrase 'sexy times,'" he said, sitting down, his leg grazing hers, "is way better than decent."

She laughed again and seemed to relax. She hit a button on the remote control and he leaned back against the sofa and watched the fictional lives of people who talked way too fast in a town called Stars Hollow. As far as he was concerned, Stonecreek could give the show a run for its money as far as nosy neighbors and everyone knowing everyone else's business.

"Don't let Jason or tonight derail you," he said after a few minutes.

Maggie glanced up at him. "How can I not?"

"You're strong." He put an arm around her, gathering her close, profoundly grateful that she was letting him into her life again. She was vulnerable tonight, which might have something to do with it. Maybe tomorrow her guard would be up again. Hard to say. But he'd take this and anything else she was willing to give. "Stronger than you give yourself credit for, and you're dedicated to the town."

"I wish it were that simple," she said with a sigh, leaning her head against his shoulder. He could smell her shampoo, and the warmth of her pressed against him made him want more. Want everything. But he tamped down his desire, because what Maggie needed tonight was a friend. Griffin wanted to be that for her.

"It is," he promised. "We're adding *complicated* to our banned list of words."

"We have a list?"

"*Sorry* is the only word on it so far, but it's a list. No apologies and no using complications as an excuse anymore."

"I like that," she whispered with a yawn.

I like you, he wanted to tell her but those three words seemed too simple to describe his feelings for

Maggie. And he'd just banned *complicated*. Where did that leave him?

As always, thoughts of the future made panic swell in his gut, so he buried them. Instead he focused on the feel of her in his arms. He brushed his fingers against her arm and she lifted a hand to his chest. His heartbeat sped under her touch, but this time it wasn't from lust. It was the odd sense of contentment of this moment, the satisfaction of being there for her when she needed someone.

Of how much he liked being that someone for her.

A few minutes later her breathing softened, becoming rhythmic in a way that made him know she'd fallen asleep. Griffin watched another episode of the show, finding himself craving a cup of coffee and a cheeseburger.

Finally he lifted Maggie into his arms and carried her upstairs. She snuggled against him but didn't wake as he pulled back the sheets on her bed and lowered her to the mattress. He tucked the covers around her, kissed her cheek and walked out of the room.

To his surprise, her dad was waiting at the bottom of the stairs.

"I wanted to make sure I didn't have to kick you out of the house," he said groggily, rubbing a hand across his eyes.

"No, sir," Griffin told him. "I just thought she'd sleep better in her bed than on the couch."

Jim nodded. "She had to grow up too fast after her mom died. Maggie's used to taking care of everyone else. It's not easy for her to lean on someone."

"I get that."

"It means something," Jim continued, stifling a yawn, "that she let you in tonight."

Griffin nodded, not sure how else to respond.

"Don't mess it up again," the older man told him simply.

"I'm going to try my best," Griffin promised.

Jim studied him for a long moment and then nodded. "You turned out all right, Griffin."

"Thank you, sir."

Griffin let himself out the front door, inhaling the crisp night air. For months he hadn't been able to shed the massive weight on his chest. But it suddenly vanished. He drove back to the vineyard and his room above the barn and slept better than he had in ages.

"You don't have to come out here with me," Maggie said, glancing at her sister as they drove toward Harvest Vineyards on Wednesday afternoon.

"What if Mrs. Stone is mean to you?" Morgan demanded, fiddling with the seat belt strap. "Everyone in town is talking about Trevor being a cheater. That can't make her happy."

"She's not going to be mean," Maggie said, although she wasn't exactly confident about Jana's reaction to the new revelation. Griffin had said his mom was angry with Trevor, who definitely deserved it. But it had been Maggie's choice to take the blame. She saw how wrong that was now, allowing her shame to manifest into a lie. "But I'm glad you're here. I want to spend more time with you."

Morgan gave a harsh laugh. "That should be easy since I'm grounded forever."

"Not forever," Maggie countered, turning up the winding drive. "How are things going with your friends?"

"What friends?" Morgan demanded. "I can't even text, so how am I supposed to have friends?"

"You're at school every day."

That earned an exaggerated eye roll. "Jocelyn and her crew don't exactly spend much time at school."

"Seriously?" Maggie blew out a breath. "I don't understand why you picked that group, Mo."

"It was easy," her sister admitted. "They seemed fun and cool and they let me in."

"Do you still feel that way?"

Morgan shrugged. "I take the SAT in a few weeks. I actually care about college, unlike most of them."

"I can't tell you how happy I am to hear it."

"Yeah, I know. You've been worried, but I'm okay, Maggie. I will be."

Maggie wanted to trust her sister. She loved Morgan and her independent spirit, even when it led to questionable behavior.

"Do you think Dad will unground me to go to the homecoming dance?"

"Has someone asked you?"

"No," Morgan muttered. "But if that doesn't happen, I could go with friends."

"I don't know—"

"I'm not talking about Jocelyn," Morgan interrupted. "There's a group of yearbook staff girls who are talking about going together. They don't get into trouble. You were probably one of them in high school."

"I did my time on the yearbook staff," Maggie admitted.

"Would you talk to Dad? Make a case for me?"

Maggie pulled the car to a stop in front of the tasting room and looked over at her sister. "It's hard for me to trust you. I want to but—"

"I promise, Maggie." Morgan's voice was pleading. "I'm trying to make friends with better kids but it's hard when I can't do anything."

"Fine. I'll talk to Dad."

Morgan unbuckled her seat belt and leaned over the console for a hug. "You're the best, Mags. Don't pay attention to any of the haters around here, and definitely not Grammy. You do your own thing. It's what Mom would want."

Tears sprang to Maggie's eyes and she blinked them away. "You do your own thing, too, Mo-Mo. Don't let anyone make you feel like you're not enough just the way you are." She ruffled her sister's hair, which Morgan had let fade from dyed blue back to her natural caramel color. "Especially Grammy."

They climbed out of the car and Morgan drew in a sharp breath as she looked at the restored tasting room building. "I'm still so embarrassed."

"The space is better than ever," Maggie assured her. "I think you helping with gala preparations will mean a lot to Jana."

Morgan made a noncommittal noise low in her throat.

"Plus it will help me sell the ungrounding to Dad." Maggie gave her sister an encouraging nod. "You're facing your mistakes and trying to turn things around." She draped an arm over Morgan's shoulders and led her forward. "We might be shopping for homecoming dresses in the very near future."

"What about you?" Morgan asked suddenly.

"You want me to chaperone?" Maggie grinned. "I'd be—"

"No way. I'm talking about the reunion dance. Isn't this your ten-year mark?"

Maggie dropped her arm. "Yes," she agreed slowly.

"I thought the old-school dance was a big deal for you this year."

"Um…I guess." Maggie tugged her bottom lip between her teeth. Morgan was right in theory. Each year Stonecreek High School held an alumni reunion dance the night before the homecoming football game. The event was a fund-raiser for the school and had become popular with graduates who'd stayed local or were returning for the homecoming festivities. The classes with milestone reunions made the dance the cornerstone of their celebration. "I've never gone before and wasn't planning on it this year, either."

"But you have to," Morgan argued.

Maggie laughed, trying for airy, but the sound came out more like a croak. "I didn't go to one homecoming dance in high school," she reminded her sister. "Dancing really isn't my thing."

The truth was she'd never been asked and hadn't had a group of girlfriends going without dates to join. She hadn't exactly been a social butterfly in high school. Between schoolwork, watching over a younger Morgan and Ben, and the community projects her grandmother had pushed her to volunteer for, Maggie had been way too busy for a normal teenage life. She'd wanted one, but she'd also been quiet and studious. Most of her classmates had labeled her a snob or too good for them, even though she'd never felt that way.

She'd come out of her shell during college and hoped she'd changed the town's perception of her once she'd returned to Stonecreek, despite what Jason said. But there was something about the high school, and the reunion dance in particular, that brought back all of her old insecurities.

"I bet Jason Stone will be there," Morgan said, eyes narrowed, "probably schmoozing with everyone and acting like he's so great."

Maggie pressed her fingers to her chest, which suddenly felt tight.

"Then he better not let anyone see him dance."

Maggie whirled around to find Griffin standing behind them, a smile tugging one corner of his mouth.

"Jason can't dance?" Morgan asked, grinning.

"Not unless he's taken lessons since his sister's wedding. She got hitched a few years ago in Portland. Jason looked like an uncoordinated Tasmanian devil when he hit the dance floor."

"Maggie can dance," Morgan offered. "Grammy made her take ballet classes back in the day."

"Not the same kind of dancing," Maggie muttered.

Morgan crossed her arms over her chest. "I've seen you dance. You have a surprising amount of rhythm for such a dork."

"I'm not a dork."

Griffin laughed. "Let's see those 'moves like Jagger,' Maggie May." When she only glared, he laughed harder. "Or are they moves like jaguar?" He growled and made clawing motions with his hands.

"You're a bigger dork than she is," Morgan said, pointing at Griffin.

"I'm wearing a tool belt," he pointed out, jiggling the leather encircling his waist. "I can't be considered a dork if I have a tool belt. There's some kind of rule."

"It's pretty hot."

"Eww," Morgan said, nudging her arm. "TMI for sure, Mags."

Maggie grimaced. "Sorry. I meant to think that, not say it."

Morgan plucked the seating chart out of Maggie's hands. "I'm going inside to start moving tables." She stepped in front of Griffin and her shoulders went stiff. "I need to tell you again how sorry I am, Griffin. I get that you don't have much of a reason to believe me, but I'm sorry about the tasting room and the fire and...everything."

Maggie held her breath as they both waited for his response. "Your dad told me you worked all summer to pay back some of the money he gave me for the damages."

Morgan nodded. "I couldn't cover all of it," she admitted, "but I've basically been his indentured servant for months. Every penny goes to that."

"I appreciate it," Griffin told her. "You might have heard something similar happened when I was your age."

"You and your friends were out here drinking and a cigarette caused the fire."

"Yeah," he whispered, running a hand through his hair. Maggie could tell he liked discussing his mistakes about as much as Morgan did. "I didn't stick around to make amends," he said. "That's part of why I'm back here now. It says a lot about your character that you took responsibility for what you did." He inclined his head. "Cole was willing to take the fall."

"I'd never let him do that," Morgan answered without hesitation.

"That shows character, too. I misjudged you after the fire, Morgan. I'm sorry."

"You were right about me back then," Morgan whispered and it broke Maggie's heart to see her sister wipe at her cheeks. "But I'm trying to do better."

Griffin gave her an encouraging smile. "That's all any of us can do."

"Thanks," Morgan said and headed into the tasting room.

Maggie watched her walk in and then moved toward Griffin.

"I think your sister and I are square now," he said.

Instead of answering, she placed her hands on his broad shoulders, went up on tiptoe and kissed him.

Chapter Seven

"Want some help?"

Morgan jumped at the sound of Cole's voice in the quiet space, tripping over a chair and landing on her back end on the floor.

Mortification poured through her as she scrambled to her feet. "Way to scare me half to death," she said, glaring at him as he grinned. "You think that's funny?"

"It was like you thought I was some demented clown coming after you," he said, stifling a chuckle, but not very well.

"Not the clown part," she muttered. "For sure demented."

"Sorry," he said, his voice and his gaze gentling. "Are you okay?"

Why did he have to be so darn cute that he made her heart race and all her defenses fade away? No. Morgan squeezed shut her eyes and shored up her walls. He'd pretty much told her he didn't like her. He'd given the stupid excuse of not being good enough for her. But it was only an excuse.

"I'm fine." She dusted off her palms, then winced. Turning over her hand, she noticed a small piece of wood embedded in the fleshy pad.

"What is it?" Cole took her hand before she could pull it away.

"A splinter." She tugged but he didn't let go. "I'll take care of it when I get home."

"We have a first-aid kit here," he told her, his work-roughened hand encircling her wrist. His skin was warm against hers and sent tiny sparks shooting down her spine.

"I don't need it." She yanked her arm out of his grasp and pinched the skin with her uninjured hand. It stung but the splinter didn't pop out.

"Don't be stubborn."

"I'm not stubborn."

"Afraid?"

She glanced at him sharply. His expression remained sympathetic and slightly challenging.

"No," she breathed even though she was afraid far too often. Not of a stupid splinter. But most everything else. Afraid of being alone, of not having friends, of the crowd she'd worked so hard to fit in with discovering she wasn't really as cool as she acted. Afraid of disappointing her dad and Maggie—although not Grammy. Disappointing Grammy was a given.

"Seriously, Morgan." Cole's voice was more insistent now. "You're freaking me out. Let's just take care of the splinter. Please."

"Fine," she whispered, sick of arguing for the sake of arguing.

He put a hand on the small of her back, guiding

her to the bar on one side of the tasting room. The space felt different than it had when she'd been here before, more open somehow.

"Stay here," Cole told her. "I'll be right back."

He was acting like the injury was serious and while Morgan knew a splinter was almost nothing, she couldn't help but enjoy the attention. It was the kindest he'd been to her in ages.

Maybe she should have faked a sprained ankle. That would have garnered some big-time sympathy. She swallowed back a guilty giggle at the thought. This was her turning over a new leaf, she reminded herself. Honest Morgan. Straight-as-an-arrow Morgan.

Cole returned, holding a white plastic box with red lettering. "I try to clean up the place every night, but Griffin's still working on the wall behind the bar and there's always sawdust and bits of wood flying."

"This isn't your fault." She reached for the box but he nudged her hand away.

"I've got it." He frowned, studying her. "You look pale. Do you need to sit down?"

"It's a *splinter*," she reminded him.

"Right." He took an individually wrapped antiseptic wipe from the first-aid kit, opened it and then dabbed at her palm.

She sucked in a breath at the sting.

"I'm hurting you," he whispered.

"It's fine."

He nodded, then finished cleaning the wound. He pulled tweezers from a plastic case and dabbed at the ends with the wipe. "What are you doing at the vineyard anyway?"

"Helping Maggie arrange the tables for the fundraiser this weekend."

"Your sister has been working on the event for a while. I haven't seen you in the mix before."

"I didn't really want to come back here," she admitted. "It's too embarrassing knowing I caused Griffin so much extra work."

"It was an accident," he said quietly.

"A stupid one." Morgan felt color heat her cheeks as she thought about that night and her clumsy attempts at seducing Cole. What did she know about seduction? A boy had kissed her only once in her life—Brady Rechtin in fifth grade. His teeth had clinked hers and he'd tasted like cheese puffs. Not a great memory.

"Everyone makes mistakes," Cole told her. "I'm sure Griffin understands."

"I think he does." Morgan shrugged. "So I guess it's good that I came today. I don't have to keep trying to avoid him. Plus I didn't want Maggie to be alone. Did you hear about what happened at the debate? How Jason Stone went after her so hard?"

"My brother's girlfriend was there," Cole answered. "She said Maggie freaked out and accused Trevor of cheating on her."

"It wasn't an accusation. Maggie caught him right before they were supposed to get married. That's why she walked away from the wedding."

"Harsh," Cole murmured. "You might want to look away. It's in there pretty deep, so I might have to dig around a bit."

A small groan escaped Morgan's lips. She really wished she would have waited until she got home to deal with the splinter. It felt so odd to have Cole fussing over her like this. She turned her head away from him, taking in the tasting room in its entirety.

It was cooler than she remembered from that one night. Rustic shiplap covered two of the walls while the others were painted a muted gray color. The ceilings were vaulted and a huge wrought iron chandelier made a perfect centerpiece for the airy space. Although tables filled the room, it still felt open and large. She could imagine tons of great events out here with the breathtaking view of the fields out the long bank of windows on one side.

She gritted her teeth as she felt the tweezers press against her skin but kept still. She was a lot of things but a wimp when it came to pain wasn't one of them.

"Got it," Cole said a few seconds later.

She turned back to see him holding up a short sliver of wood. "All that trouble for something so small," she said, taking the antiseptic wipe from the counter and pressing it to her palm again.

"It wasn't any trouble," he assured her, his voice warm and gentle.

She was such a sucker for gentle.

"Delilah…my brother's girlfriend," he explained, "said a couple of her friends think Maggie's just making up the business about Trevor cheating to make the Stones look bad again."

"That's not true," Morgan said, feeling her temper swell. "She'd never do something so underhanded."

"I didn't say I believed it." He put away the tweezers and snapped the box closed. "Delilah is kind of a bi—" He paused, took a breath. "She likes to gossip and can get pretty nasty."

"How are things at your house?" Morgan asked

quietly, then almost regretted the question when Cole stiffened. She knew he didn't like to talk about his family and all the trouble his dad and brother seemed to attract.

"Dad's not drinking as much lately," he said finally. "And mainly sticking to beer instead of hard liquor. That helps."

"Oh." She didn't know how to even begin responding to that.

"Sorry you asked?" He gave a harsh laugh.

"I'm not." She placed her hand on top of his and squeezed. "I'm glad things are getting better. You deserve that."

"Do I?" The notion seemed to surprise him. "What about you? How's your dad?"

"Still taking an interest in me," she said, "which is equally nice and annoying." When he gave her a pointed look, she sighed. "Okay, it's more nice than annoying. It's going pretty good, actually. Maggie said she'd help convince Dad to let me go to the homecoming dance."

He pulled his hand from hers. "So you can sneak out of it and hit the party circuit with Jocelyn and her loser group?"

"No." Morgan crossed her arms over her chest. "I just want to go the dance."

"Who's your date?" he demanded, his tone chilly. "Zach or Jonah?"

Zach and Jonah were two of the guys who ran with the wild group of juniors and seniors she pretended were her friends. Both were total meatheads and not at all potential date material as far as Morgan was concerned. She shook her head. "I wouldn't go with either of them."

"That's smart at least. Then who?"

"I don't have a date," she whispered. "No one has asked me."

"Someone will."

"I doubt it." She stepped away from the bar, glancing at the seating chart she'd taken from Maggie. She needed to act casual so Cole didn't think she was fishing for an invite. Because she wasn't. Not even a little bit. "I'll probably go with girlfriends."

"I'd ask you."

The words were spoken so quietly, Morgan wasn't even sure she'd heard them correctly.

She turned to him. "You would or you are?"

He stood on the other side of the table, staring at her like he still couldn't figure out what she was doing there.

"You already know I'm no good for you." His voice was rough and pleading, as if having this conversation was physically painful for him.

"That's not true." She gripped the edge of the table, moving it several inches to the right, needing something to distract her from the intensity of Cole's gaze. "You keep saying that, but I think it's just an excuse because you're not interested in me." She threw up her hands. "I get it, Cole. Fine. I never said I wanted you to ask me in the first place. Forget this whole conversation even happened. I'm going to find Maggie."

Swallowing back the pain from another rejection, she started for the door. Why did she keep torturing herself with a boy who was clearly not at all interested in her?

Before she took two steps, warm hands grasped her arms. Cole turned her to face him. His hands moved up until he cupped her cheeks. Then he leaned in and kissed her.

Morgan's breath caught in her throat. Although it wasn't anywhere near how she'd planned it, the kiss was the most perfect thing she'd ever experienced.

His lips were soft against hers and it felt like she was being engulfed in a tornado of butterflies. She wanted it to go on forever, but all too soon he lifted his head.

"You taste like mint gum," she murmured.

Cole tucked a strand of hair behind her ear, a half smile playing at one corner of his mouth. "Is that good?"

"Very good. Way better than cheese puffs."

His grin widened and Morgan realized she was babbling about how he tasted. She might not be super experienced, but she knew enough to understand that was not what a girl was supposed to do after a boy kissed her.

"You taste like the stars at midnight," he told her, his voice low as if he were sharing a secret.

Her heart seemed to skip a beat and she totally forgot her embarrassment. "That's not a thing."

"It's our thing," he countered and she loved the sound of that. "I know that I'm supposed to make some big production of asking, but I don't want to wait. If your dad says it's okay, will you go to homecoming with me, Morgan?"

"Yes," she whispered and then he kissed her again.

* * *

Griffin wrapped his arms around Maggie, slanting his head to deepen the kiss. As their tongues mingled, it was difficult to know where she ended and he began. He wanted to stay like this forever.

Finally she pulled away, her lips swollen and her chest rising and falling like she'd just run a marathon. From the way his heart raced in his chest, he imagined he looked much the same way.

"See how simple that was?" she asked with a laugh, and he couldn't tell whether she was talking to him or to herself.

"I was thinking more along the lines of *amazing*," he told her, "but *simple* works, too."

She laughed again.

"I missed that sound," he whispered, pulling her closer. "I missed you, Maggie May."

But before he could kiss her again, the sound of a truck engine could be heard coming up the driveway. She shifted out of his embrace, taking several steps away from him and smoothing a hand over the front of the pale gray shift dress she wore.

An older-model Chevy pulled to a stop in front of the tasting room and Thomas Helton, Harvest's cellar manager, got out. "Hey, Grif," the man called. "Marcus asked me to stop by and check the barrels they brought up here for the gala."

"No problem," Griffin shouted back, turning to Maggie as Thomas disappeared around the side of the building.

"What was that?"

She frowned. "Nothing."

"You jumped away from me like we were teenagers with your dad about to catch us in the back seat."

"Well, I don't know what this…" She waved her hand between the two of them as if fanning the flames of a bonfire. "What this is right now. Until we figure it out, I want to keep it private."

Irritation flickered along the back of his neck. "What's there to figure out?"

She chewed on her bottom lip, clearly thinking about how to answer. Overthinking, as far as Griffin was concerned. Never a good thing.

"There's going to be backlash from the debate," she said finally. "The campaign will kick into high gear in the next couple of weeks. I have the gala to get through and you're almost finished with the tasting room."

"Which means?"

"You tell me," she shot back. "The last I heard, you were heading out once the renovations were complete. You've paid your debts and all that. Has something changed?"

Yes, he wanted to shout. He'd changed. She'd changed him. But the words wouldn't form. "I don't know."

"Then we need to keep things simple," she said, almost sadly.

"Yeah," he agreed reluctantly. But his body and his heart screamed in protest. Simple was never going to be enough with Maggie, but he wasn't sure how to give more. It had been so damn long since he'd tried.

"I'm going to check on Morgan," she said after a

moment. "Thank you for coming over last night. It meant a lot to me."

"Go to the reunion dance with me," he blurted.

She stilled. "Excuse me?"

"The dance," he said slowly. "A date. You and me."

"You don't go to high school dances."

"Not in high school," he admitted. "But it's different now." He took a step closer to her. "I'm different."

"Griffin."

"Don't make me beg, Maggie." He rubbed his thumb over her bottom lip. "But I will if that's what it takes. It'll be the perfect night. You and me and some cheesy dance moves. I understand your need to keep your private life private, but it's your ten-year reunion. You have to go."

"You don't."

"I want to. I want to be with you."

She sucked in a breath, then whispered, "Okay."

"I'll get you the biggest corsage you've ever seen," he promised, unable to hide his grin.

She smiled back at him. "That might be pushing it."

"The white tux I'm already planning is pushing it." He stepped back and did a few impromptu dance moves, ending with an elaborate twirl.

"Who are you right now?" Maggie asked with a laugh.

The man trying to win your heart, he thought, but only bobbed his head again, feeling like John Travolta in his *Saturday Night Fever* days when she clapped and wolf whistled.

"Stop!" They both turned as Morgan and Cole came out of the tasting room. Morgan made a face and held up her hands to shield her eyes. "My corneas are burning," she shouted.

Cole pointed at Griffin, holding his stomach with one hand as he threw back his head and laughed. "Worst dancer ever."

"Punk kids," Griffin muttered, narrowing his eyes. "You can do better?" he asked Cole when they got closer.

"My two-year-old cousin can do better," the boy told him.

"Don't listen to them. You were great." Maggie beamed and Griffin didn't care if the whole damn world criticized his dancing. All that mattered was making her smile.

"Cole and I got the tables rearranged."

"Thank you," Maggie said, and he noticed the boy blush under her scrutiny. "We should get going," she said to Morgan. "I need to check with the florist about the centerpieces."

Morgan glanced at Cole, then gave a little wave.

He waved back, coloring a deeper shade of pink.

"I'll talk to you soon," Griffin told Maggie.

"Sure," she agreed, still grinning. "I'll have the image of you dancing in my mind for the rest of the day."

Morgan groaned.

"Lucky you," Griffin told her and watched the two sisters get into Maggie's car and drive away. "What are you smiling about?" he asked Cole when they were alone.

"I asked Morgan to homecoming."

"Nice work, buddy." Griffin gave the boy a

friendly slap on the back. "I'm taking Maggie to the reunion dance."

"Dude." Cole nudged his arm. "Right back at you."

"You own a suit?"

"Um…no. But I can—"

"We'll drive into Portland tomorrow after school. I need a tux for the gala anyway."

"You don't have to do that," Cole muttered.

"I know," Griffin agreed. "But if I offer *you* up to the salespeople, they'll hopefully ignore *me*."

"Rude."

"You dissed my dancing."

"You really suck."

"Maggie doesn't think so."

Cole snorted. "She was just being nice."

"I'll take nice," Griffin said softly and saw Cole nod.

"Me, too," the boy whispered.

Chapter Eight

"I think you should wear the black boatneck."

Maggie turned from the mirror on the back of her closet door to meet her grandmother's sharp gaze. "You look pretty," she said, pasting on a bright smile.

"That dress is suggestive," Grammy answered, ignoring the compliment. Her eyes zeroed in on the deep V of the neckline. "Are you even wearing a bra?"

"There's one built into the dress," Maggie explained, resisting the urge to roll her eyes at Grammy's disapproval. The dress was totally appropriate for the hospital fund-raiser. With no time for a shopping trip into the city, she'd ordered it online and been ridiculously pleased when it fitted. The fabric was a shimmery silver, with tiny beads sewn in intricate rows. Although it had a plunging neckline, the rest of the dress was more demure with capped sleeves and a hem that fell below her knees.

"It's scandalous for someone in your position," Vivian said, shaking her head.

"Grammy, the dress is stylish and quite conservative compared to some of them. I love it."

"Me, too," her father said, coming to stand next to Grammy in the doorway of Maggie's bedroom. "Leave her alone, Mom." He dropped a quick kiss to the top of Grammy's head, which the older woman tried to wave away. "She looks beautiful."

"Well, of course she's beautiful," Vivian said with a sniff. "She could wear a potato sack and be gorgeous. I just thought she'd want to be seen in something more modest after her most recent scandal. I don't want the haters to have any reason to talk about you, Mary Margaret."

Although couched in judgment, Maggie knew her grandmother cared about her. "I'll be fine, Grammy."

"Want me to grab a rusty knife from Dad's studio?" Ben ducked into the room between their father and grandmother. "I still haven't gotten to shank anyone."

He flopped down on the bed, arms and legs flailing like he was making a snow angel.

"You'll wrinkle your suit," Grammy warned.

"Then maybe Dad will let me change," he shot back.

"No chance." Jim tugged at his starched collar. "Misery loves company and all that."

"Who's miserable?"

Maggie heard Morgan ask the question from the hallway. Their dad stepped back to allow her sister into the room.

"Oh, my." Grammy put a hand to her chest as she stared at Morgan.

Morgan grimaced under the scrutiny. "What did I do now?"

"You look absolutely stunning," Vivian murmured. "So much like your mother."

"Um...thank you," Morgan whispered, fiddling with the material on her A-line, chiffon-lace dress in a deep midnight blue. She seemed shocked to be on the receiving end of Grammy's approval in any way.

Tears sprang to Maggie's eyes. Morgan did indeed favor their mother, with her light hair and peaches-and-cream complexion. Although it had been over a decade since their mother's death, there were times when Maggie felt the loss like a fresh wound, raw and painful.

Jim cleared his throat. "All three of my girls are gorgeous, not to mention my handsome son. That makes me a very lucky man."

"I'm hardly a girl," Vivian said with a delicate snort, if a snort could be described as delicate.

"You're a beautiful lady, then," Jim conceded.

"That's right, Grammy." Morgan wiggled her eyebrows. "You better watch the fellas tonight. Someone may try getting fresh given how hot you look."

"Don't worry," Ben added, hopping up from the bed and executing a complex series of ninja-like moves. "I can—"

"If you use the word *shank*," Grammy said, holding up a hand, "we're going to have problems, young man."

"I'll pop him in the family jewels," Ben offered instead with a cheeky grin.

Maggie laughed as Grammy rolled her eyes. As difficult as her family could be, Maggie was grateful for each one of them at the moment.

She felt far too nervous about tonight's event.

She'd kept a low profile in the past week with the excuse of needing to finalize details for the gala. But she really hadn't wanted to face the fallout from her revelation at the debate with Jason. Brenna had assured her that most people were in her corner, but Maggie wasn't convinced.

"Let's go," she told everyone, and they filed down the stairs and out to her father's Volvo station wagon.

Maggie's nerves increased as they got closer to the vineyard. They were arriving early to help with any last-minute preparations, so at least she'd be able to stay busy before the guests began to arrive.

Jana greeted them at the door of the tasting room. "This place looks even better than I imagined," she said with a smile, gesturing everyone into the building.

Maggie's breath caught as she took in the space. All of the details she'd agonized over for weeks had come together to create a magical setting. She'd chosen a scheme of autumn colors, paying tribute to both the season and the vineyard's name. The tables were covered with linens in deep shades of russet and gold, and strands of party lights had been hung above the bar, giving the space a warm glow. Light still streamed in from the picture windows onto vases arranged with sunflowers, hydrangeas and seeded eucalyptus that gave a festive look to each of the tables.

A server dressed in black offered her a glass of wine from the tray he held. "This vintage has been carefully aged in our winemaker's private cellar and opened specifically for the event," he said. She'd known Harvest had created a special label to sell tonight with the proceeds going to the hospital foundation, but she hadn't had a chance to sample it yet. She sipped the wine. The fruity flavors of ripe cherries and crushed berries exploded on her tongue.

"What do you think?" a deep voice asked from behind her.

She turned to find Griffin watching her. His gaze dipped from her face to her dress, then back up again.

"Wow," he murmured. "You take my breath away."

Pleasure bubbled up inside her at the compliment. "The space is amazing," she said. "You did such a good job."

"Thanks." He adjusted the collar of his black tux, much like her dad had earlier. "It's been a while since I climbed into a monkey suit."

"You're very handsome tonight," she said, looking at him through her lashes. His hair was combed away from his face and still damp at the ends, like he'd just showered. He was clean-shaven and filled out the tuxedo like he was auditioning for the role of a Pacific Northwest James Bond. Not that Griffin needed fancy clothes to be drop-dead gorgeous. It was a given with him. But formally dressed he looked almost out of place in Stonecreek, as if he'd just stepped out of a New York nightclub or off a movie set.

"But not as good looking as me, right?" Trevor came to stand next to Griffin, giving him a playful punch on the arm. "I mean, his tux is rented. What kind of man doesn't own his own tuxedo?"

"The kind who never wears one," Griffin ground out, clearly annoyed at his brother's intrusion.

"You look great, too," Maggie said, offering Trevor a tentative smile. They'd exchanged a few texts since she'd blurted out what he'd done, but this was her first time seeing him in person.

"It's okay, Mags," he said and leaned in to hug her. "I deserved it."

"My intention wasn't to hurt you," she said, needing him to hear the words. Needing to speak them.

Trevor nodded, but she saw Griffin's mouth thin.

"I wanted to keep my word, but Jason made me so angry. I'm—"

"Don't apologize," Griffin interrupted gruffly. "You have nothing to be sorry about." He turned to his brother. "Nothing," he repeated.

"Got it," Trevor muttered. "She also doesn't need you to defend her against me. I'm not the bad guy in this situation."

Griffin laughed without humor. "You keep telling yourself that."

"Tasting room looks great, Grif." Trevor's eyes narrowed. "When are you leaving town?" He inclined his head toward Maggie. "You know he's still planning to take off?" he asked her.

She opened her mouth, shut it again.

"Mind your own business, Trev."

"I've dedicated my career to Harvest Vineyards," Trevor shot back. "It is my business. A couple months of dipping your toes in the water around here doesn't make you committed."

Griffin glared. "Thanks for the reminder. I need to talk to Marcus." He gestured to where the CEO stood on the other side of the room, then turned and stalked away.

"Brotherly love," Trevor murmured, taking a glass

of wine from a nearby server and draining it in one gulp. "We bring out the best in one another."

Maggie could see guests beginning to arrive but she didn't move. "Does the animosity between the two of you have anything to do with me?" She colored as she asked the question. It felt ridiculous to think she had the power to have that kind of effect on either of the Stone brothers, but she couldn't help but admit they were all a part of some wonky, misshapen love triangle.

Trevor was silent for several long seconds. "I want you to be happy," he said finally. "I care about you, Mags, and I know I messed up your life pretty badly. Letting you take the fall for why we canceled the wedding was probably the worst. It was a cowardly move, and I like to think I'm better than my actions."

"You are."

He shrugged. "Apparently not. If Griffin makes you happy, I can live with that. But be careful. I know how charming my brother is. It comes easy to him. What doesn't come naturally for Grif is sticking around when things get complicated."

Maggie's mouth went dry. Griffin had admitted as much to her in the spring. She wanted to believe he'd changed. That his time in Stonecreek and the connection between them was enough to make a difference. He hadn't said the words, but she'd felt it when he'd held her...when they'd kissed.

"He's not the same as he used to be," she said, but the words rang hollow even to her own ears.

"We'll see," Trevor answered. He leaned in and brushed a kiss against her cheek. "Be happy, Mags."

She nodded, wiping under her eyes as unexpected

tears filled them. She wanted to be happy. Why did it feel like such an elusive goal? As Trevor moved away, Maggie's gaze snagged on Griffin, standing next to Marcus. He watched her with a frown and she wondered if he'd seen Trevor's friendly kiss and what it meant to him. Would they ever get past everything between them and simply focus on fostering their undeniable spark?

Grammy called to her then, and Maggie made her way to the entrance of the tasting room to help greet attendees for the night's event.

She was swept into a tide of gala business, talking to big donors and helping people find their seats. To her surprise, the few people who brought up her outburst during the debate were women. All of them seemed sympathetic to the reasons she'd chosen to hide Trevor's cheating in the first place.

It was a shock but somehow the knowledge that she'd been betrayed seemed to garner a strange kind of sympathetic connection with her. She realized that her grandmother's insistence on always presenting a perfect image in public didn't actually help Maggie. Maybe it had worked for Vivian and her generation, but in the era of social media and constant oversharing by people in the public eye, Maggie understood she'd do better just being herself.

The relief she felt realizing she could take a break from the arbitrary standards she'd set for herself was like slipping off a pair of uncomfortable heels at the end of the day. She'd always been more of a comfy shoe kind of girl anyway. It was time she stopped worrying so much about her image and started focusing on the work she wanted to get done as mayor.

She sat with her family during the dinner, happy to see that both Morgan and Ben seemed to be enjoying themselves. She hoped her younger brother held tight to his sunny disposition through his teen years. Maggie wasn't sure she could handle another recalcitrant teen, although Morgan had smiled more in the past week than she had in months. That had a lot to do with Cole, who was working as one of the busboys for the formal dinner.

"Jana tells me he's a decent kid," her dad murmured, as if reading Maggie's mind. "Your sister can't seem to stop with the cow eyes."

"I don't think they're called cow eyes anymore," Maggie told him, taking a sip of wine. "She's crushing on him."

Her dad made a noncommittal sound in the back of his throat. "And I'll crush him if he hurts her."

"Look at you being the overprotective father," Maggie said, nudging his arm.

"I'll do the same for you," he offered. "I noticed you talking to both Griffin and Trevor earlier. How was that?"

"Awkward," Maggie admitted. She leaned closer. "Speaking of noticing, you seem to be spending an awful lot of time tonight glancing in Jana Stone's direction."

"Impertinent child," her father muttered under his breath.

Maggie looked at him more closely, surprised to see that he seemed to be blushing. "Dad?"

He darted a glance at her, then trained his gaze back to his dinner plate, which appeared to hold the most fascinating piece of chicken he'd ever seen.

"Is there something between you and Griffin's mom?" Panic skittered across Maggie's neck at the thought. There were enough complications between her family and the Stones without adding one more.

"Before your engagement to Trevor, I'd barely spoken two words to Jana in the past thirty years."

Not exactly a definitive answer to her question.

"What about thirty years ago?"

"A lifetime," he whispered and stabbed at an asparagus stalk.

"Not quite. Do you have a history with her?"

He lowered his fork to the plate and sighed. "Stonecreek is a small town. I have a history with almost everyone here."

"Yes, but—"

"She's thinking of commissioning a piece for the entrance of the winery. We've been discussing ideas."

"Oh." Maggie nodded. That made more sense. "Do you have time in your schedule?" Her dad's bronze sculptures were popular, and each one took him months to complete.

"Maybe." He took a drink of wine and grimaced.

"Dad." Maggie slapped his arm, glancing around to make sure no one had seen him. "You can't make that face at the vineyard."

"Give me a cold beer any day," he told her. He put down the glass and turned fully to Maggie. "I told Jana we could talk after the election. I want to devote the next couple of weeks to you. Canvasing, making phone calls, whatever you need. Hell, I'll even make an appearance at one of your grandmother's awful Historical Society meetings if you think my presence could help."

"Thanks, Dad," Maggie whispered.

"I'm not exactly the political expert my mother is," he admitted, "but I've lived here all my life and everyone knows me. I can twist arms with the best of them."

She chuckled. "Hopefully no arm twisting will be needed, but I appreciate the support."

A hush fell over the room at that moment as Georgia Branson, the president of the hospital board, took the microphone in front of where the band had set up. "Thank you all for coming tonight," she said with a smile. "I'm so pleased to tell you we've raised sixty-five thousand dollars toward our new pediatrics wing at the hospital." There was a polite round of applause and she nodded. "I'd also like to publicly recognize the two people who have been instrumental in making this gala such a success."

She pointed toward the back of the room. "Jana Stone, your generosity in donating this beautiful location, your time and the wine is appreciated by all of us."

"Especially the wine," someone shouted and the crowed laughed.

"Maggie Spencer," Georgia continued, "your creativity, organizational skills and out-of-the-box thinking have made this the most financially successful fund-raiser we've ever had."

Maggie smiled and cupped her hands to either side of her mouth. "It was a whole committee effort," she called.

"Our esteemed mayor is too modest," Georgia told the audience. "Some of us had our doubts about a Spencer and a Stone being able to work together, but these two ladies have put aside family drama…" She tipped the wineglass she held toward Maggie, a bit of golden liquid sloshing over the side.

"Is she drunk?" Grammy hissed from across the table.

"I mean, who would have guessed Mary Margaret Spencer was such a drama queen?" Georgia tittered and then took a long swig of wine.

"Add her to the shanking list," Ben said.

"Stone for mayor," a feminine voice called from a nearby table. Maggie was pretty sure she recognized Emily Stone, Jason's wife, as the heckler.

"Shank her, too," Grammy told Ben.

Maggie felt like her cheeks might crack as Georgia waggled a finger toward the guests, more wine spilling over the side of the glass. "No politics tonight," she cautioned. "We're all here for one goal. Maggie has done a great job of getting us to that goal, despite her mess of a personal life."

Maggie sucked in a breath and felt her father squeeze her numb fingers. She looked down at where their hands were joined and was enormously grateful for the contact. Her smile remained frozen in place and her cheeks burned from the weight of the stares she could feel pointed in her direction.

Suddenly there was feedback coming from the speakers and she heard a faint grunt.

"Okay, then, folks." She glanced up to see Griffin holding the mic as Trevor led a frowning Georgia toward the edge of the room. "That was a…uh… spirited speech by our hospital board president and a great reminder that while Harvest Vineyards makes fantastic wines, enjoy them in moderation."

A few laughs greeted his words.

She could see his chest rising and falling as the room quieted once again. Griffin might have grown up in Stonecreek, but she knew he still felt like an outsider, even at the vineyard. Making himself the center of attention wasn't easy, and the fact that he was doing it for her made her heart skip a beat.

"Seriously, though," he continued, as if realizing he hadn't quite adequately defused the situation, "both Maggie and my mom have gone above and beyond for tonight." Another round of applause. He nodded, then said, "This night is particularly special to me because it marks the unofficial reopening of the Harvest Vineyards tasting room." More clapping. "Thank you. This building was special to my dad and, as most of you know, he and I didn't always have the closest relationship when I was a kid." He held the microphone closer and leaned forward, as if imparting a great secret. "Mainly because I was such an idiot."

"We love you," Jana called from the back of the room.

Griffin smiled. "Thanks, Mom. Thanks for giving me a chance to make things right here. I don't know what Dad would have thought of this, but I hope it would have made him as happy as it's made me."

He looked toward the members of the band. "It's time to let these guys do their thing, and I hope you all are wearing your dancing shoes. Although I've been told recently that I'm not exactly Fred Astaire, I'm going to kick things off." He took several steps forward and Maggie's breath caught as he pointed to her. "Maggie Spencer, may I have this dance?"

Once again she could feel all eyes on her, only this time it was easier to ignore whatever curiosity or judgment might be coming her way and focus on Griffin. It felt as if he was aligning himself with her, publicly claiming her for all to see.

Her heart soared as she stood and walked toward him. And when she slipped her hand into his, it felt like coming home.

Chapter Nine

Griffin blew out a breath as he handed the microphone to the bandleader. The strains of a Frank Sinatra song began and he pulled Maggie into his arms. For a brief, terrifying moment, he'd thought she might refuse to dance with him.

"So much for keeping things private," she whispered, smiling up at him.

"Are you mad?" He glanced around, relieved to see other couples joining them on the dance floor.

Her hand curled around the back of his neck, some of the tension easing at her gentle touch.

"I think this is another case of you rescuing me," she told him. "Now instead of people talking about my messy personal life, they can speculate on what's going on between the two of us."

"You don't need rescuing," he assured her, "and I'm done with guessing games." He leaned in and brushed his lips over hers.

She tensed and he thought she might pull away.

"Don't go," he pleaded.

"Everyone is watching."

"Let them." He splayed his hand over her back. "You're beautiful tonight, Maggie. You're also smart and funny and dedicated to this town. I get that. I also understand what's at stake for you in the next couple of weeks. But I want to be a part of your life for real, not just sneaking around when no one is looking."

"But you said—"

"Forget what I said. How I feel about you is simple. I care, more than I have for anything or anyone in a long time."

"Griffin."

"All the other stuff isn't going away. I get that. This is what matters to me. I'm not going to stand by and let people take cheap shots at you. I know you can handle it. You're stronger than most people know. But I don't want you to have to handle it alone."

She stared at him for several seconds, like she was searching for something…some kind of answer. "Okay," she said finally.

He blew out a breath and grinned. "See how simple that was?"

"Simple," she agreed and rested her head against his shoulder as they danced.

Griffin closed his eyes and swayed to the music, reveling in the feel of Maggie in his arms. It was a shockingly liberating feeling to have claimed her so publicly. Maybe tomorrow would bring real life crashing back in, but for now this was all he needed.

As the music ended, he took her hand and led her through the crowd, nodding and smiling to the people who offered words of encouragement. Support he'd take and the rest of the town could go to… Well, he had plenty of experience ignoring people who didn't support him.

The night was crisp and clear as they stepped out into it and he drew in a deep breath, feeling the band around his chest loosen now that they were away from the curious eyes of the town.

"That was intense," she said, pressing a hand to her cheek.

"Are you okay?"

She nodded. "It's strange. For years I've been in the public eye in Stonecreek. Even as a kid, my grandmother loved to trot us out for ribbon cuttings and town events, living proof of her place in the community. I don't remember how my mom felt about it, but I know Dad hated it. Morgan, too. And Ben was too little and easygoing to care. I was the one who made the effort to be the person she wanted people to see." In the moonlight she could see his brows furrow. "It was never really me. I think walking away from the wedding was the first thing I've ever done just because I wanted to."

"I'm glad you walked away," he said, unable to pretend he felt any different.

She glanced over her shoulder and flashed the faintest wisp of a smile. "Me, too, but it changed everything. I don't want to go back to being the well-behaved puppet I was before that, but discovering who I want to be now isn't the easiest thing to do in the middle of an election."

"You've said before that you followed in your grandmother's footsteps because it was expected. You were the chosen one in your family." He moved closer, reaching out and trailing one finger against her bare arm. "Is being the mayor really want you want, Maggie?"

"I want to make a difference in this community," she said, which wasn't exactly an answer to the question. "I love this town."

"There's a whole big world out there that you won't see if you're stuck here."

A shiver passed through her and she turned to face him. "I don't think of it as stuck. Do you?"

He shook his head. "Not anymore."

That answer seemed to please her because she moved forward and wound her arms around his waist. "Thank you for asking me to dance tonight."

He chuckled and kissed the tip of her nose. "Thank you for saying yes."

Voices filtered out into the darkness and he shifted so they were more fully in the shadows.

"That was well worth a check to the hospital," a male voice said, and Griffin felt Maggie stiffen in his arms.

"Vivian could only keep that girl under her thumb for so long," a woman answered. "It's about time the Spencers learned that they're human just like the rest of us."

"Seems like our oh-so-perfect mayor is not only human but also damned hot after those Stone boys. If she can't hang on to one, she'll settle for the other."

Griffin took a step forward, but Maggie held him back. "Don't," she whispered. "They aren't worth it."

He growled low in his throat instead of answering because the words he wanted to say would have made his army buddies blush. Closing his eyes, he dipped his chin until it rested on the top of Maggie's head.

He breathed in her fresh scent and flowery shampoo like it would calm him.

Car doors shut and a moment later an engine roared to life and he glanced out to see brake lights disappear down the winding drive.

"What's wrong with people?" he asked.

She shook her head. "They're petty and insensitive. But not all of them."

"Enough of them to make me want to be a hermit," he told her, smoothing the hair away from her face. "I'm sorry you had to hear that."

"No apologies." She placed a finger on his lips. "Remember?"

"Do you want to go back in?"

She shook her head. "You heard the donors. The event is a success. My work here is done."

"What about your family?"

She sighed. "I guess—"

"Maggie?" Morgan walked toward them from the entrance.

"Hey, Mo-Mo." Maggie stepped away from Griffin. "Did you need me?"

"I saw you two sneak out," the girl said, "and I thought you might need this." She held up a small black clutch.

"My purse." Maggie took it, then hugged her sister. "How's it going in there?"

"Old people dancing," Morgan reported, then glanced toward Griffin. "Some of them worse than you, which is pretty bad."

"You never even saw my best moves," he told the girl.

"Lucky me," she said with a laugh, then turned

to Maggie. "I guess you're not coming back to the party?"

"Can you tell Dad and Grammy?" Maggie asked.

Morgan nodded. "I think Mrs. Branson is already puking in the bathroom. She's going to feel real bad about her speech, especially after Grammy gets through with her."

"I can't say I feel that bad for her," Maggie said with a sniff.

"I like this new you." Morgan stepped away from Maggie with a grin. "You're all *Kill Bill* tough."

"Let's not go too far," Maggie answered and hugged the girl again.

When Morgan returned to the tasting room, Maggie held up her purse. "I'm all yours," she whispered.

"And well worth the wait," he told her, lacing his fingers with hers. "I walked over from the barn." He glanced at her strappy heels and made a face. "Do you want me to get the car and pick you up?"

She bent, pulled off her shoes and held them up as they dangled from two fingers. "I'm ready."

"Then let's make a quick trade." Griffin shrugged out of his tux jacket, draped it over Maggie's shoulders, then took the shoes from her. "I'll hold these and you stay warm in that."

He took her hand again and they made their way across the expanse of lawn that led to the barn and upstairs apartment.

"It's so peaceful out here," Maggie murmured, pausing to glance up. "The stars never cease to amaze me."

"I feel the same way about you," he said and drew her close, unable to resist kissing her again. The need and desire he'd tamped down these past few months roared to life. It was all he could do not to pull her down to the grass and strip off that sexy-as-hell dress to reveal every inch of her.

A breeze kicked up and he felt her shiver, even within the warmth of his jacket. "Inside," he told her and they almost ran the rest of the way to the barn and his apartment above.

As soon as Maggie was up the steps, Griffin lifted her into his arms, pressing her back to the wall next to the door. He fused his mouth to hers, hoping to tell her everything he still couldn't put into words. Things he barely understood about his heart and how it felt like she'd brought it back to life.

Her fingers tangled in his hair as he trailed kisses along her jaw, down her throat and then across her collarbone, tugging the delicate fabric of her dress off her shoulders. But before it fell completely, he lifted his head, his gaze zeroing in on the pale skin revealed at the center of the dress's deep V-neck.

"Did you pick this outfit just to make me crazy?" he asked gruffly.

She breathed out a husky laugh. "No, although I hoped you'd like it."

"I'm obsessed," he admitted, "with everything it revealed and the promise of what was hidden." He bent his head and licked the skin between her breasts. "I imagined kissing you here all damn night."

She moaned and pushed her head back against the wall. "Anywhere else?"

He laughed. "Oh, yes." He tugged the dress down her arms, leaving her naked from the waist up. Then he sucked one taut nipple into his mouth, making her moan again.

"More," she whispered, and he loved her willingness to take command of the moment. Of him. He kissed and nipped and sucked first one breast, then the other, wondering if he'd ever get enough of the taste and feel of her.

Her hands went to his shoulders, kneading the tight muscles there. He straightened, yanking on his bow tie. "I need you to touch me," he said as he undid the buttons of his crisp white shirt.

"I like the sound of that," she told him with a saucy smile. She shimmied out of her dress, the fabric pooling at her feet and leaving her in nothing but a pair of black lace panties.

"Going to kill me," he managed to rasp through gritted teeth, his fingers fumbling on the button of his tailored slacks, "in the best way possible."

Maggie looked up at him through her lashes. "I haven't even done anything yet."

"My point exactly." When he'd stripped down to only his boxers, he picked her up, groaning with pleasure as her legs wrapped around his waist. Her hot center pressed against his erection, sending desire rocketing through him.

"I've missed you," he said against her mouth, moving toward the bed that sat against one wall. The apartment was, in essence, a studio—a loft-type room with a small kitchen in one corner, a couch and television situated a few feet away. The bed was at the far end of the space on the opposite wall.

It wasn't exactly impressive and for the first time Griffin thought about renting his own place in town, much like Trevor did. Or buying a house. He stumbled a step, then righted himself.

"You okay?" Maggie asked, cupping his cheeks between her warm palms.

"Yeah," he whispered and kissed her again. One thing at a time, he reminded himself.

This moment—here with her—needed to be his only focus.

Not hard to do as he laid her down on the bed, stretched out across his sheets, her thick hair fanning over his pillow like he'd imagined so many times in his fantasies.

He shoved his boxers down over his hips, then leaned over her to hook his fingers in the waistband of that amazing black lace. One side of her mouth curved up and her gaze darkened, as if she liked watching him strip her down.

It was the most erotic moment of his life, his breath coming out in short pants, and there was so much more. It was difficult to believe this beautiful, intelligent, caring woman had chosen him…had risked her reputation for him. Griffin didn't know how to tell her what it meant to him, but he damn well planned to spend all night showing her.

He opened the nightstand drawer and pulled out a condom packet.

"Let me," she whispered and took it from his hands. A moment later her fingers moved down the length of him and Griffin sucked in a harsh breath.

"Killing me," he repeated, then moved over her on the bed. He claimed her mouth at the same time he drove into her in one long thrust, and he wondered how he'd ever been able to walk away from this woman. She was everything.

It was funny to Maggie that Griffin kept talking about death, because to her being in his arms, in his bed—the moment so intimate it felt as though they were one—was like coming alive in a whole new way.

Yes, she'd been with him months before and it had been amazing. But this—now—was different. She was different and Griffin… Something had changed in him, making hope spring to life inside her.

Her body tingled from head to toe as pressure built through her body. With each thrust, each kiss, passion wound around her until she was consumed by it. He whispered her name between kisses and she moaned low in her throat when he reached between them to touch her.

It was too much and everything she'd ever imagined all at once. Desire spiraled and then splintered, sending shock waves of pleasure through every cell. A few seconds later Griffin stiffened, then moaned his release, and she wrapped her arms more tightly around him, loving the gift of sharing this moment.

Loving him, although she understood at some intrinsic level that it was too soon to utter the words.

So she concentrated on breathing normally and smoothed the hair away from his forehead, beaded with sweat from his exertion. He levered himself up on his elbows, cool air rushing across her skin as he stared down at her.

"Amazing," he whispered, his gaze intense on

hers, and Maggie was grateful he felt the same way she did.

Then disappointment snaked around her gut, not at him but herself. What did it say about her that she was grateful a man thought she was decent in bed? Not much, unfortunately.

"What?" he asked, one finger skimming over the line she knew had formed between her eyes. "Tell me that was good for you."

She frowned harder at his words. "Are you joking? You have to know how good you are. I can't imagine you've made it this far without hearing it at least a thousand times."

He shifted so he was next to her on the bed, propped up on an elbow. "A thousand may be pushing it," he said with a grimace. "Besides that, what happened between us wasn't just me, Maggie. It was you, too. Both of us together. I know enough to understand how special our chemistry is. Don't you?"

"Yes," she said softly. Chemistry. Physical chemistry. Was that what he thought made this so mind-blowing?

"Did I do something wrong?" he asked. "It feels like something shifted between us just now and not for the better."

She shook her head, leaned in and kissed him. "Of course not. You did everything right. More right than I realized was possible."

"Good. I'll be right back." He rolled away from her, grabbed his boxers and headed toward the far end of the studio apartment. She could see the bathroom through an open door. He closed it and she heard the sound of running water.

She stretched across the bed and reached down to grab a discarded T-shirt, pulling it over her head and then snuggling into the covers. She felt surrounded by Griffin in this bed, enveloped in his scent, her body still warm and pliant from the pleasure he'd given her. But the dull ache in her chest wouldn't ease. Fear and doubt crept in and tried to crowd out everything good about this moment.

As Griffin returned to the bed, Maggie did her best to put all of that aside. Everyone wore a mask, she told herself, and it was dangerous to let him see what was behind hers. She'd played a role for so long, how could she stop now?

"Oh, great," he murmured, wrapping his arms around her and pulling her to his chest. "You're dressed."

She snorted. Unladylike and probably the opposite of what a man wanted to hear from a woman in his bed, but she couldn't help it. "What's that supposed to mean?"

"Well, for one…" His big hands skimmed along her waist and hips, then moved under the shirt. "The sight of you in my shirt is beyond sexy." He kissed her and even though she'd thought her body completely satisfied, need and desire rose to the surface once again. "And two, I've decided my new favorite hobby is undressing you." He shifted her, gently prodding her legs open. "Now I get another chance."

She made a little noise of satisfaction, which seemed to be exactly the reaction he wanted. Within minutes they were both naked and sweaty again, and Maggie buried her fears and doubts under the satisfaction she found in Griffin's arms.

Chapter Ten

The scent of freshly brewed coffee woke Maggie the next morning. She blinked and pushed the hair out of her face, glancing at the unfamiliar ceiling above her.

"This is why I need more than one room. Sorry I woke you."

She sat up at the sound of Griffin's voice, pulling the covers with her.

"I'm naked," she whispered, then clasped a hand over her mouth when a strangled giggle escaped.

"Which is funny because?" Griffin asked the question as he approached the bed, holding out a mug of steaming coffee to her. He wore a Harvest Vineyards T-shirt and low-slung basketball shorts. His dark hair was tousled and a rough shadow covered his jaw. It was difficult to believe he could be hotter than he'd looked in the tux—or in his birthday suit for that matter—but Maggie thought he'd never been more handsome than at this moment.

Maybe it was the affection in his eyes as he looked at her. "Well?" he prompted.

She shrugged, reaching for the coffee with one

hand and using the other to keep the sheet tightly clasped above her breasts. "I don't sleep naked," she said with another giggle.

"As I remember," he told her, sitting on the edge of the bed, "there wasn't a lot of sleeping."

"Right." Maggie sipped from the coffee mug, then glanced at the clock. "I should go. It's bad enough I'm going to be doing the walk of shame into my dad's house. I don't want to be out here if anyone stops by." She rolled her eyes. "Like your mother."

Griffin leaned in and kissed her. He tasted of coffee and toothpaste and her body immediately heated. "No shame, although you're motivating me to get my own place."

"Me, too." She sighed and rested her forehead against his. "I wish we could stay in bed all day."

"That's the best idea I've heard in ages."

She shifted away when he moved closer. "Don't tempt me."

"That's what I'm here for," he told her with a laugh.

"But now you have to turn away," she said, shoving at his chest. "I need to get dressed."

"A reverse striptease." One thick brow lifted. "Sounds intriguing."

"No way." She placed the mug on the nightstand. "Thank you again for last night."

"Which part?" He tapped a finger on his chin, as if in deep contemplation mode. "When you were on to—"

"Defusing the situation at the fund-raiser. You rescued me."

He shook his head. "I've already told you I'm not

the hero type, and you're strong enough that you don't need rescuing. But I'm happy to be in your corner. Always."

"I love you," she whispered without thinking, then wished the floor would swallow her up. "I'm sorry," she added immediately. "I didn't mean it." She pressed a hand to her flaming cheek. "Well, I meant it, but I didn't mean to say it out loud. Not now. You don't have to say anything back. It's too much—"

"No apologies." Griffin leaned in for a soft kiss, then lifted his head to look at her. "You are the best thing that's happened to me in a long time, Maggie."

She returned his smile, although a sharp twinge lanced her heart when he didn't say those three words back. But he'd claimed her at the gala, in front of both their families and most of the town. That counted for something. A lot.

"I'll go start the car," he told her as he straightened. "But next time I'm holding you hostage in bed all day."

She rubbed at her chest when he walked away, then quickly got dressed. The words she'd uttered and his reaction to them replayed over and over in her mind. Was she confusing great sex with true emotion?

No.

She wouldn't believe that. Even if Griffin couldn't say the words yet, she knew he cared about her. She believed it was even more than that. It had to be. Their connection was too strong for any other explanation.

They talked about inconsequential things as he drove her to her father's house. Normally she loved their easy banter, but this morning it felt stilted, like they were filling the silence to avoid her premature declaration.

She forced another smile when he pulled to a stop at the curb.

"I'll call you later," he told her, leaning over the center console for one last kiss.

"Okay," she whispered and let herself out of the car, hurrying up the front walk in the soft light of morning. The street was empty and she said a silent prayer that none of her dad's neighbors were glancing out their windows this early.

The house remained quiet and she managed a quick shower and change of clothes before anyone woke. Her father was in the kitchen when she came back down the stairs.

"Late night?" he asked, raising a brow.

"Yeah," she agreed, reaching for the coffeepot. "You know how it goes."

He gave a noncommittal grunt in response. "I didn't see you at the event after the first dance."

"I slipped out for some air," she told him. "It got a little intense."

"I'm sure you'll be receiving a call from Georgia as soon as she remembers—"

"It's fine," Maggie lied. "At some point this town will get sick of talking about me."

"You're a Spencer," her dad said with a humorless laugh. "I doubt it."

"You manage to stay off the radar."

"Look at what it cost me." He pressed his hands to the counter. "I relied on your mother to do most of the heavy lifting as far as parenting, and when she died, a lot of that responsibility transferred to you. I didn't know how to deal with life in this town other than to hole up in my studio."

"You did the best you could," she told him.

"Which was pretty inadequate."

"Dad."

"I know." He shrugged. "I'm trying to do better. In the spirit of my more active dad role…" He picked up a flyer from the counter and held it out to her. "We're having a family fun day today."

"The pumpkin patch," she murmured, taking the slip of paper from him.

"It's got a corn maze, too," he said with a nod.

"I'm not going through a corn maze," Morgan announced as she came into the kitchen. "It freaks me out."

"Scaredy-cat," Ben said, following on her heels.

"You're both going," Jim announced, pointing between the two of them. "And you're going to like it. We're bonding."

Maggie thought about adding her two cents about how he was a decade too late for this kind of forced family fun, but at the hopeful, almost pleading look her father shot her, she couldn't manage it.

"The pumpkin farm is outside Corvallis," she told her brother and sister. "We can have breakfast at Annie's Cafe on the way."

"Seriously?" Morgan asked with an eye roll. "You think this is a good idea?"

"Sure." Maggie forced a cheery tone. "It will be a new family tradition."

Morgan snorted. "It's a little late for traditions."

"It's never too late," Maggie said with more confidence than she felt.

"And no cell phones," their father announced, earning disbelieving sounds of protest from each of them. "No arguments. We're going old-school like your old man."

"You'll survive," Maggie said, feeling like she needed to support her dad when he was trying so hard. "Cell phones in the basket on the table. You'll be reunited with them again when we're back home. Go get dressed. We leave in fifteen minutes."

Both Morgan and Ben grumbled but dutifully placed their cell phones into the wicker basket in the center of the table that held mail and other odds and ends from their daily lives.

"I'm going to change into sneakers," Maggie told her dad. "Then I'll be ready."

"Cell phone," he responded.

"Oh." She frowned, pulling the device from her back pocket. "I was hoping you didn't actually mean me."

"I mean all of us." He plucked his from the counter and put it with the others.

Maggie's fingers tightened around hers. "I'm in the middle of a campaign, Dad."

"It's Sunday."

She fidgeted under his stare. "I have to follow up with some things from last night."

"They'll wait," he said calmly.

Maggie sighed, then gingerly placed her phone on top of the others. "You're not joking about this family bonding stuff."

"It's as strange for me as it is for you," he assured

her. Then he wrapped an arm around her shoulder for a quick hug. "Getting away will be good for all of us. We need a break."

She couldn't argue so she reached up and kissed his cheek. "My goal for the day is to beat Ben through the corn maze."

He laughed. "Good luck with that."

Maggie not only failed to beat her brother through the corn maze, she'd gotten so lost that Ben had to retrieve her. She might never live down her lack of direction, but the laughs were worth the grief she took.

The day had been perfect. With no real-life distractions, the four of them had fun as a family. They took turns trading stories of Halloweens past and all the last-minute costumes Jim had put together for them.

Planning was definitely not his strong suit, although the spontaneous family outing—even though it seemed a little late in coming—had to be one of his better ideas.

They'd stopped for breakfast at one of Maggie's favorite diners on the way, then ate hot dogs and roasted s'mores over the bonfire at the pumpkin patch. There were farm animals to pet and a hayride, and Maggie had as much fun as any of the little kids milling about. Sipping apple cider, she watched the families with young children, imagining what it would be like to someday bring her own sons or daughters to the pumpkin patch. She imagined a little boy with big green eyes and rumpled hair, then sucked in a breath, choking on the juice.

Griffin hadn't even been able to say he loved her

back and already she was imagining kids who looked like him. She needed to slow down in a big way.

She concentrated on the moment and her family. The ride home in the golden light of the fall afternoon was picturesque, and it felt like weeks' worth of emotional baggage had been lifted from her shoulders.

Until they pulled up to the house.

"What's Grammy's car doing here?" Ben asked warily.

Morgan groaned. "She's on the porch waiting for us."

Maggie's stomach lurched. "I have a feeling she's waiting for me."

"I'm sure she hasn't been here long," her father said, reaching over to pat her leg. "The timing is probably a coincidence."

"We could keep driving," Morgan suggested in an overly bright tone.

"It's fine, Mo-Mo." He parked next to the white Lexus in the driveway and Vivian was already halfway across the yard by the time Maggie climbed out of the front seat.

"Where have you been?" She pointed at Maggie. "Why are none of you picking up your phones?"

"We went to a pumpkin patch," Jim said with a smile, coming to stand next to Maggie. "And left our phones at the house. Come to think of it, I should have asked you to join us on the outing. We got an extra pumpkin so you can come over for carving later this—"

"Did you know about it?" Grammy demanded,

coming to stand in front of Maggie, eyes blazing. "Did Griffin tell you first?"

"Tell me what?" Maggie forced her features to remain even.

"The planned expansion at Harvest," her grandmother said through clenched teeth. "A boutique inn and reception hall. It's a full-out assault on the Miriam Inn and our events center. They're trying to cripple our business. They're out to ruin us."

"Mom," Jim said calmly, "let's go in the house and discuss this. I'm sure it isn't as bad as you're making it seem."

"Did you know?" Vivian repeated the question to Maggie.

"No," Maggie admitted. "I have no idea what you're talking about."

Grammy studied her for several long seconds, then finally nodded. "At least you haven't betrayed me completely, despite some of the questionable decisions you've been making in town recently."

Maggie swallowed, licked her dry lips. "I've been trying to do what's right for the community," she argued, hating that her voice trembled. "The whole community."

Vivian sniffed. "You need to remember on which side your bread is buttered, young lady."

"I never understood that saying," Jim murmured.

"Grammy, don't threaten Maggie." Morgan crossed her arms over her chest and took a step forward.

"No sass from you." Grammy's focus switched to her younger granddaughter. "You're a child. You don't understand the workings of Stonecreek the way I do." She threw up her hands. "None of you get it. I've devoted my whole life to this town…to this family."

"We know that, Mom," Jim said quietly. "We appreciate everything you've done but—"

"They're trying to usurp our position," Grammy said, her voice cracking. She looked away like she needed a moment to compose herself. "I promised my father that I'd make him proud." Her gaze swung back to Maggie. "He hated that I wasn't a boy. He thought I'd never make anything of myself because I was too weak." She wiped hard at her cheeks. "But I showed him. I married your granddad and with the Spencer family's backing, the Miriam became far more than it had ever been with my father running it. I made him proud, although he was hard-pressed to admit it until the day he died."

She looked at each of them. "I won't have all of our success—my accomplishments—undone by that family of upstarts. People who forget their place."

"Grammy." Maggie placed a gentle hand on her grandmother's thin shoulder. "Everyone knows how much you've done for Stonecreek, but things aren't like they used to be. I'm sure the plan at Harvest Vineyards isn't going to ruin your business."

Vivian narrowed her eyes. "We'll be second-rate." Her chin trembled. "I'll be second-rate. Just like my father always told me."

Maggie's chest ached at the pain in her grandmother's tone.

"Mom, come in the house," Jim urged gently. "Let's talk about this. It can't be as bad as you—"

"I have to go," Vivian said with a sniff, unwilling to make eye contact with any of them. As if she

was embarrassed about the tiny cracks of vulner-
ability in her steely tough-as-nails armor. "I have a
meeting with Steve Brage from the zoning board.
He owes me. Maggie, I'll call you at the office tomorrow. This is town and family business. We need
to make a plan."

She stalked to her car, climbed in and drove away
without a backward glance.

"That was intense," Ben said, kicking at the grass.

"I've never seen Grammy like that," Morgan
added. "It's almost like she was human for a few
minutes."

Their father shook his head. "Of course your
grandmother is human."

"Can we have our phones back now?" Ben asked,
displaying the typical empathy and focus of a teenage boy.

"Sure," Jim agreed and both Ben and Morgan took
off for the house.

"I bet I missed more snaps than you," Ben said
to his sister.

"In your dreams," Morgan shot back.

"You knew nothing about the plans at Harvest?"
Maggie's father asked when they were alone in the
front yard.

She shook her head. "Did you know Grammy had
that relationship with her dad?"

"No," Jim admitted. "She's always been a force
of nature, but I thought it was just family pride. My
grandparents died when I was a kid, and she seemed
more interested in the Spencer legacy than my dad
was. I never questioned why that was."

"I need to talk to Griffin," Maggie murmured almost more to herself than her father. "I can't believe he wouldn't have shared those plans with me."

"It could be a game changer." Her dad ran a hand through his hair. "Not that I think it's as dramatic as your grandmother makes it out to be, but it will lessen the control she has over local businesses and she hates losing control."

"I know," Maggie agreed, then gave her dad a hug. "Coming home to this mess makes me even more grateful for today. Thanks, Dad."

"What the hell is this about?"

Jana, Marcus and Trevor turned in unison as Griffin stormed into the conference room in the winery's office early Monday morning.

"You're late," Trevor muttered. "As usual."

Jana sent her younger son a withering look. "Sit down, Griffin. We're just getting started."

Griffin slammed the business section from *The Portland Chronicle* onto the oak table. "Is this a joke?" He jabbed a finger at the headline Stonecreek Winery Expands Empire. "Why didn't I know about this?"

"None of us did," Marcus said tightly, his mouth set in a thin line.

"Well, I did," Trevor offered. "I wrote the press release, after all."

"This is going to directly impact the Spencers' business interests in town. You know how Vivian thinks. She'll take it as a personal attack. Are you trying to start a war with them?"

Trevor snorted. "Don't be a drama queen, Grif. This is business."

"Bad business," Griffin said, meeting his mother's worried gaze. "This came as a shock to you?"

Her brow wrinkling, she looked away with a sigh. "Not completely. We'd discussed the possibility of building a venue on the property." She held up one finger when Trevor opened his mouth to speak. "But nothing had been decided. The plan had been to meet with the Spencers and some of the other business owners in town to determine how we could complement what was already established downtown."

"My opinion," Marcus said, drumming his fingers against the table, "was that Harvest Vineyards should continue to focus on what we do best." He leveled a stony look at Trevor. "Which is making wine."

"This is about expanding the brand," Trevor argued. "And in the end, selling more wine. It's a win for all of us." He glanced at Griffin. "Except maybe those of us needing to suck up to Vivian Spencer."

"I'm not sucking up to anyone," Griffin said through clenched teeth. He paced to the far side of the room where a window framed a view of the rows of vines below. "Stonecreek is a small town and—"

"Yeah," Trevor interrupted. "We live here, Grif. None of the rest of us has the luxury of just dropping in when it suits our fancy."

"No one forced you to come back here after college." Griffin whirled around. "You made that choice all on your own."

Trevor lifted one brow. "Did I?"

Their mother rose from her chair. "Stop arguing. Both of you." She inclined her head toward Griffin. "Your brother is well aware of the vineyard's place in this community." Her gaze switched to Trevor. "You should also be aware that although you have quite a bit of autonomy in leading the marketing and branding efforts for Harvest, this is not a dictatorship. I remain sole owner of the business and Marcus is CEO."

"For now," Marcus murmured.

Griffin felt his mouth drop open at those two words. Trevor looked equally stunned, but their mother only sighed.

"Please sit down, Griffin. We have a lot to discuss."

"Are you leaving Harvest?" Trevor asked Marcus.

"We'll get to that in a minute," Jana said in the tone she'd relied on when the boys were young to put a quick end to any back talk. "Sit, Griffin."

He dropped into a seat like a puppy following the command of his human in obedience class.

His mom reached across the table and pulled the newspaper toward her. "Trevor, the next time you create a press release for the vineyard, send it through me first."

"Mom, come on. I'm not a kid."

She lifted her gaze and stared icily at him. "Then don't act like one. We'd talked about an event center that would enhance what was already available in town, not compete with it."

"I'm sick of kowtowing to the Spencers," Trevor complained. "I understood the reasoning while I was dating Maggie, but there's no connection to them now."

Trevor threw a glance toward Griffin, as if daring him to speak. Clearly, Trevor's moment of wanting Maggie to be happy had passed like a fleeting sunset.

"We have a connection," Jana said before Griffin

could respond. "This town is our connection. Our history is the connection. I won't have you using the vineyard as a way to work out personal vendettas."

"I'm not doing that," Trevor insisted. "It's good business."

"Not your call to make," Jana said simply. "As Marcus alluded to, he's decided to step back from some of his responsibilities at Harvest. He's agreed to stay on in a consulting role but as of the first of the year, he'll no longer be our CEO."

"Why?" Griffin demanded. "You love this place."

"I do," Marcus agreed. "But now I have something in my life I love more. I want time to devote to Brenna and Ellie."

Griffin shook his head. "How can it be that serious? You just started dating her a few months ago."

"I let my professional aspirations derail my personal life once before." Marcus sat back in his chair, leveling an almost challenging look toward Griffin. "I'm smarter than that now."

"Who gets the job?" Trevor asked, leaning forward.

"That's what we're here to discuss," Jana said, her voice giving away nothing. "You can see why your premature announcement comes at a difficult time, Trevor."

"That doesn't change anything." Trevor crossed his arms over his chest. "I should be the next CEO, of course."

"You've done so much for the brand," Jana agreed, "but whoever takes over needs to be able to juggle the various facets of the business."

"I can do that," Trevor told her.

"But do you truly want to?" Jana asked. "Is Harvest in your heart?"

Griffin's chest constricted at her words. Despite Marcus's encouragement, he hadn't really believed he had a place at the vineyard. Not after everything that had happened with his father and how he'd reacted. It was difficult to believe anyone would give him a chance to prove he deserved a place in the family business. But the vines were in his heart. He knew that without a doubt.

He glanced at his brother, surprised to see color tingeing Trevor's cheeks as he stared at his mother, hands clenched into tight fists on top of the table. "How can you ask me that?" he demanded. "I've made this place my life. I came back to Stonecreek, the way Dad expected. I gave up everything for him."

"I know, sweetie," Jana said gently. "Everyone knows."

Wait. What? Griffin didn't know. He could feel the undercurrent of tension at the table but had no idea where it came from. Trevor had everything Griffin had ever wanted—especially their late father's love and approval. What was his damn problem?

He met his brother's icy glare across the table. It felt as if Trevor blamed Griffin for whatever was going south right now. Impossible because Griffin hadn't been a part of any of it.

"I earned my shot," Trevor said, enunciating each word, launching them like rockets toward each person in the room. Before anyone could respond, he pushed back his chair and stalked away, slamming the door behind them.

Griffin looked between his mother and Marcus,

who exchanged worried glances with each other. "Let me repeat my original question," he said when neither of them spoke. "What the hell is this about?"

"We want you to take over the vineyard." Marcus steepled his hands and leaned forward, his warm brown eyes intense on Griffin. "Your mother and I have been making plans for this since you came home."

"Before that even," Jana added.

"Was anyone going to mention it to me?" Griffin pushed away from the table, much like his brother had minutes earlier. Instead of following Trevor out of the room, he approached the far wall to the collage of framed photos of the property over the years. There was a photo of his great-great-grandfather, who had first farmed the land, a few aerial shots of the fields and photos of the various expansions over the years.

The largest photo hung in the center of the wall and showed his dad and mom toasting each other with the first pinot noir they'd bottled. He and Trevor stood on either side of them. Griffin smiled broadly—he could still feel the excitement of that first day, but Trevor was frowning at the camera. As Griffin remembered it, they'd had to cancel a family trip to the Grand Canyon because his dad had barely left the vineyard those first couple of years. Griffin had never minded, but his brother had hated all the things they'd missed because of the family business.

"What about Trevor?" he asked, turning to his mother. "He's right about everything he sacrificed for Harvest. I got to have a life away from here. He's been tied to the vines for his whole life. Don't you think he's earned his place at the helm?"

Her mouth tightened. "Of course he has, but it isn't about that. I want him to be happy. I want both of you to be happy." Her eyes shone with unshed tears as she looked up at him. "Trevor doesn't want to leave for the same reason you don't want to come back. Your father." She sighed. "I know he did his best, but if he could have known how things would end up here—"

"He wouldn't have changed a thing," Griffin interrupted. "I'm sorry, Mom, but it's true. Dad only cared about the way he saw things. I was the screwup and Trevor was the golden child. There was no room for any middle ground in his world."

"It isn't his world any longer," she said with a sniff. "I want you to take over for Marcus. I want you to run Harvest."

Griffin ran a hand over his face. Those were the words he'd always longed to hear, but now he had such a clearer understanding of the significance of what a commitment like that meant. "I appreciate your faith in me, and I'll think about it." He wasn't sure why he couldn't just say yes, but something held him back. Something that sounded a lot like his father's doubting voice.

His mother didn't look pleased by his response but she nodded. "I'll talk to your brother," she told him.

"What about his big plan for an event center and inn?"

"We're not ready for that," Marcus answered. "I'll make sure Trevor understands why."

"It's a good idea," Griffin said quietly. "Other

vineyards have expanded to great success. It would make Harvest a destination if it's done right."

"Are you saying you support his plan?" Jana asked.

"No," Griffin admitted. "I'm saying it's smart for the business if the goal is to keep expanding." He met Marcus's knowing gaze. "But I agree that it's not where we want to be right now. Harvest needs to focus on our environmental certifications and making the best wine we can. Anyone can be the biggest. We should be the best."

"I'm glad to hear you say that." Marcus nodded. "It confirms why your mother and I believe you should be the one to take over my position."

"We'll have to find a way to pull back from Trevor's public announcement without embarrassing him."

"Of course," Jana agreed.

Griffin sighed. "I'm still not sure about this. I wasn't joking when I said I needed time to make a decision."

"You've been concentrating on rebuilding the tasting room," Marcus told him. "I know we've had a few conversations about the future of the vineyard and you were here for the harvest this year. But you need to understand the state of the business right now. Work with me for a week. Let me show you where things stand. Then you can decide how you want to proceed."

Griffin felt his heart speed up as he thought about really being a part of Harvest again, more than just making amends for his mistakes.

"Okay," he agreed. "I have some things to wrap up with my crew today. I'll report for office duty first thing tomorrow."

Both his mother and Marcus smiled.

"This is how it was always meant to be," Jana said. "You'll see."

Griffin walked out of the office, wishing he shared his mother's confidence.

Chapter Eleven

"Are they going to open a restaurant, too?"

"How many people will the venue accommodate?"

"Is the vineyard zoned for that kind of enterprise?"

"What are you going to do about this?"

Silence descended upon the room at that last question, lobbed by Vivian Spencer, of course. Maggie nodded as if acknowledging each of the inquires and forced her features to remain neutral. Her grandmother had called an emergency meeting of the Stonecreek downtown business association for Monday morning, and Maggie had cleared her schedule so she could attend.

Vivian wasn't the only one wary of Harvest Vineyards' proposed expansion. Many of the small business owners in town had concerns about what the news would mean for them. Although Harvest was officially in the town of Stonecreek, the property was an equal distance from the next town over, Molberry. And while Harvest was associated with the Stone family's namesake town, there had already been rumblings about the leaders in Molberry trying to ingratiate themselves with Trevor in order to become the preferred vendors for any items that needed to be outsourced once the Harvest event center and guest lodge opened.

"I left messages for Trevor and Jana," Maggie reported, not bothering to add that neither of the Stones had seen fit to return her calls yet. "I plan to set up a meeting with them by day's end so we can get a real understanding of the plan." She lifted the copy of Trevor's press release she'd printed earlier. "Details are limited in what Trevor sent out, so I'm guessing he doesn't have them yet."

"What about Griffin?" Russ Wileton, who ran Stonecreek Realty, demanded.

Maggie bristled at the accusation in the man's tone. "What about Griffin?" she shot back.

"He fawned all over you at the gala," restaurant owner Irma Cole added. "That has to mean something. Don't you have some influence with him?"

"As far as I know," Maggie said carefully, "Griffin isn't involved in this announcement." He'd sent her a cryptic text late last night that he was "working things out on his end"—whatever that meant. But that was the last she'd heard from him. Not exactly giving her warm and fuzzy feelings about their status as a couple, but she was probably silly for thinking he'd offer anything more.

"He had to know it was coming," Vivian said, her tone disapproving. "It reflects badly on all of them that we had to find this out at the same time as the rest of the world."

Maggie doubted the whole "rest of the world" was

interested in the future plans of an Oregon vineyard, although she understood it was big news in the regional wine industry. With the expansion, Harvest would be one of the most prominent wineries in the area.

"I don't think any of you have reason to worry," she said with more confidence than she felt. "Obviously we just had our most successful hospital fundraiser to date at the vineyard. Jana and Marcus are committed to this community."

"Trevor still has it out for you." Dora Gianelli, whose family had operated the bakery in town for more than three generations, flipped her thick gray braid over one shoulder. It was difficult to believe that the biggest gossip in Stonecreek looked like a sweet, harmless throwback to the Woodstock era. "You know...for standing him up at the altar."

"I remember," Maggie said through clenched teeth. "And in case I ever start to forget, I can always pop by the bakery for a slice of Runaway Bride Banana Bread." She smiled at Dora. "Don't you think it's time to go back to plain old banana bread?"

Dora shrugged. "The name change has been real popular. I'm trying to add more creative names to the desserts. Spice things up a bit."

"You could call one Cheater, Cheater, Pumpkin Pie Eater," Irma suggested with a wide grin. "In honor of Trevor. Display it in the case next to Maggie's bread."

"It's not my bread," Maggie said, throwing up her hands. "I doubt Trevor would appreciate that kind of attention, either."

"That's a good point," Dora said with a nod. "I

don't want to make the Stones angry. They've promised to increase their standing order of croissants and cookies now that the tasting room is open." She leaned toward Irma. "I give them a big discount, of course, because of all the tourists coming to the bakery after they try my stuff at Harvest."

Maggie resisted the urge to roll her eyes. No one in town seemed the least bit concerned about getting on *her* bad side.

"Do you think Jason has more pull with the family?" Russ asked, and Maggie bit down so hard on her cheek she could taste blood inside her mouth.

"I doubt it," Irma answered before Maggie had a chance to respond. "He was always a bit of an outsider, and I don't think anyone in Dave Stone's immediate family likes him. There was some bad blood when Dave inherited the farm and his brother got the time-share in Arizona."

"Also," Dora added, hitching a thumb in Maggie's direction, "Jason isn't sleeping with either of the brothers. That has to count for something."

"That's crass, Dora," Grammy muttered. "Even for you. To think Maggie would barter sexual favors for influence is insulting."

"Don't get on your high horse with me, Vivian," Dora shot back. "I remember when you dated Mark Kipling after Chester died. You can't tell me you were honestly interested in that onion-breathed weasel other than the fact that he owned the bank."

"Enough." Maggie rose from her chair, gripping the edge of the oak conference table. "I'm done having my private life carted out for inspection at every turn. I've worked hard during my first term as mayor.

I hope each of you will support me in this election because I'm good at this job."

She glanced at her grandmother and then away. "Not because of my family name or who I'm dating or because you think I'm a good sport about my fiancé cheating on me. I care about this town and I care about the members of the business community. I'll work things out with Harvest. While they're important to Stonecreek, so are each of you. You're important to *me*. I'm going to make sure we do the right thing for everyone."

"Don't worry, Maggie," Chuck O'Malley said in his gruff voice. "We've got your back."

"Thanks, Chuck." She smiled as the rest of the association members around the table nodded or called out their support. Her grandmother was uncharacteristically quiet and refused to make eye contact.

Maggie would worry about whatever bee had taken up residence in her grandmother's bonnet later. Right now, she was emotionally drained. "I'm going to get back to city hall while you all finish your meeting. I promise to follow up with Jana and Marcus and keep everyone updated."

With another sidelong glance at Vivian, who still appeared mesmerized by something Russ was saying next to her, Maggie waved to the rest of the business owners and then left the room. The Miriam Inn looked much as it had when Maggie was a girl. Personally, she thought the interior of the building could benefit from a bit of a face-lift—or at least a light freshening. But this was her grandmother's domain and Maggie wouldn't dare give Grammy suggestions on how to run her business.

The town square was quiet this Monday morning, with only a few people walking their dogs on the path and the local tai chi group practicing on the open expanse of lawn in the center. The day was overcast, although the brightly colored leaves and the fall decorations that adorned the businesses up and down Main Street still made downtown look cheery.

Maggie pulled out her phone again, but she had no missed calls from anyone at Harvest Vineyards. Disappointment lanced through her. Somehow she knew Jason Stone would spin this latest development in his own favor, and although she wanted to believe the members of the business association supported her, she wouldn't blame them for looking out for their own interests.

Her fingers hovered over the home screen, but then she shoved the phone back into her purse. She needed time to research other vineyards that also housed event venues before making her case to the Stones.

She breathed deeply as she entered city hall. Since her grandmother had been mayor for most of Maggie's childhood, the scent of pine and decades-old files was familiar and made the tension in her shoulders ease slightly. Her own personal version of a relaxation candle. It represented so much to her, and although the past months had been difficult, she didn't regret that she'd chosen to follow in her grandmother's footsteps. The key now was honoring that past while forging her own path.

She greeted several people but didn't stop moving. Right now she needed her own space and to recharge. Only her office wasn't empty. Griffin stood in front of the bookcase that lined one wall, holding a framed photo of Maggie as a baby in her mother's arms.

"Hey," he said with that almost smile that never failed to make her knees turn to jelly.

"Hi," she whispered, then swallowed when her voice caught on the one syllable.

"You look like her." He turned the frame toward her as if she didn't have the image memorized.

"She was prettier than me," Maggie answered. "Morgan is almost her doppelgänger."

He placed the frame back on the shelf. "Your sister has the same hair color, but I see you in her eyes and around the mouth."

Tears clogged Maggie's throat. She'd love to believe she resembled her mother, either in looks or personality. "I still miss her."

Griffin nodded, as if that was to be expected. "I miss my dad, and we didn't even like each other. I can't imagine how it must feel to lose someone you truly love."

"You don't fool me," she told him, moving forward. "I know you loved your dad." She reached out and laced her fingers with his. "I'm sure he loved you, too."

Griffin snorted. "I don't know about that part, but you're right on the first. I loved him even if I never could make him happy."

"He'd be proud of you now."

"My mom said the same thing to me."

"Great minds…"

He lifted their hands and kissed her knuckles. "You seem stressed."

"I just came from the downtown business owners'

association. It was an emergency meeting to discuss the new plans at Harvest."

Griffin grimaced. "I'm sorry for that."

"Why didn't you say anything?" She tried to tug her hand away, but he held fast.

"I didn't know. None of us did. Trevor and my mom had discussed the idea of an event venue, but she wanted to figure out what was needed based on what was already working in town."

"Like the Miriam Inn's conference center?" She raised a brow.

"Yes," Griffin answered without hesitation.

"You can understand why I find it difficult to believe Trevor didn't make the announcement on purpose."

"Believe it or not, I think him jumping the gun on the announcement had more to do with me than you."

"Because you're with me?"

He shook his head. "Marcus is stepping down as CEO."

Maggie drew in a sharp breath. "Brenna told me he'd said something about wanting more time to spend with her and Ellie, but I had no idea he wanted *that* much time."

"He'll be involved but not in the day-to-day operations." Griffin still held her hand, running his thumb along the fleshy edge of her palm. It was an absent touch but also intimate in a way that had butterflies fluttering across Maggie's chest. "He and my mom want me to take over."

"Not Trevor?"

His full mouth thinned. "I was as shocked as you are. Trevor is the obvious choice."

She moved closer, placed her free hand against

his chest and spread her fingers, feeling his steady heartbeat. "I'm not shocked that they want you, Griffin. You love the land and you have an innate gift for understanding the vines, just like your dad did."

"I've been gone for so long," he murmured, his eyes drifting shut as if in pain.

"I'm guessing it's like riding a bike."

One side of his mouth curved up as he blinked, then met her gaze. "Not exactly."

"But kind of?" she prompted.

"Kind of," he agreed.

"I asked about Trevor because he told me he expected it to happen."

"He's not the only one. He knows the business end and the branding better than anyone. His expertise is a big part of the reason Harvest is now a well-known player in the wine industry. It's not just regional anymore, either. He's expanded our reach, increased the export sales by over twenty percent the past two years and generated a ton of buzz about the vineyard's new varietals. Just listing his accomplishments makes me feel like a slacker."

"But his heart isn't in it," she said quietly, pressing her hand against his chest.

He huffed out a laugh. "It's like you and my mom are the same person."

"Ewwww." Maggie made a face and pulled away.

Griffin laughed again. "I didn't mean it like that, and you know it."

"Let's get out of here," she blurted.

He glanced around. "Out of your office or the town hall building in general?"

"Stonecreek," she clarified. "Can you sneak away for an overnight in Lychen?"

"My little coastal-town hideaway made quite an impression on you, huh?"

"I did love the town," she said, "but you made the impression." Lychen, about an hour from Stonecreek, was a picturesque town nestled against the craggy beaches of the Oregon coast. It had been the setting for their first date, a perfect night away from the pressures of family and community. An evening for just them, and Maggie wanted to recreate that magic.

"I'm supposed to meet with Marcus first thing tomorrow morning."

"We can come back tonight," she suggested, trying not to let her disappointment show.

"Or I could reschedule my meeting with Marcus." He closed the distance between them in two long strides, wrapping an arm around her waist and pulling her close. His mouth molded against hers and she hummed her pleasure as he deepened the kiss. Even though it had only been a day and a half since she'd spent the night at his apartment, it felt like ages ago.

"I like your plan better than mine," she said when he finally released her. Every fiber of her being tingled with need at the same time her stress from earlier melted away. The only thing she cared about at the moment was being with Griffin.

"What about a change of clothes?"

She grimaced and shook her head. "I can't go back to my dad's house. I'll get sucked into real life."

"No real life," he said, kissing her again.

"Too complicated," she answered, wrinkling her nose.

"The banned word." He clasped a hand to his chest in mock horror.

Maggie giggled as happiness filled her. Being with Griffin made her truly happy and she couldn't imagine a better reason to play hooky from life than the chance to spend the day—not to mention the night—with him.

They managed to sneak out of the town hall with no one seeing them. Maggie's car could remain parked in the employee lot behind the building, so they climbed into Griffin's Land Cruiser and headed for the coast. Maggie texted her dad, Brenna and her assistant, Megan, to let them know she had to take a quick trip out of town and would return tomorrow.

Then she turned off her phone and set it on the console, leaning her head against the seat to gaze out the window at the changing landscape.

"Why didn't we think of escaping before now?" Griffin asked with a smile.

"I'm not sure," she admitted. "Because already this is the most fun I've had in ages."

"It only gets better from here," he promised, and he was right. They stopped for a late lunch at a local deli in one of the towns off the main highway and pulled into Lychen just as the sun was beginning to make its way across the sky toward the horizon.

"Beach and then hotel," Griffin told her as he parked in a lot near the pier.

Maggie made a face as she looked down at her pencil skirt and modest heels. "I'm not exactly dressed for the sand."

"You look perfect to me," he told her as they climbed out, Maggie leaving her shoes inside the SUV.

She felt perfect, despite being overdressed. He took her hand and they walked down to the edge of the ocean. It was nearing low tide so a wide expanse of beach was exposed. The sand was cool under Maggie's feet. At this time of year, the temperatures near the coast were in the fifties and a strong breeze blew her hair in all directions.

She inhaled deeply of the salty air and leaned closer to Griffin. He slung an arm over her shoulder, the heat from his body warming her as they walked. A few pelicans hopped around the rock formations just offshore, foraging for food, but otherwise they had the beach to themselves.

Back in early summer when they'd had their first date, Maggie couldn't have imagined how important Griffin would become to her. They were an unlikely match—he with his devil-may-care attitude and the heart of a rebel and her always wanting to please everyone, even at the expense of her own happiness.

It was easy to be with him, natural in a way she'd never experienced with anyone else. There was no denying that she'd fallen head over heels in love with this man. And although she still wasn't certain if those feelings would ever be reciprocated, she couldn't help but believe he cherished the connection between them as much as she did. It had to be only a matter of time until he said those three words back to her.

Chapter Twelve

"Nice going, Spencer. Way to work the system."

Morgan swallowed as Zach Bryant dropped next to her on the lunch table bench. She concentrated on peeling the orange she'd packed and not looking at Cole, who sat across from her.

She didn't need to look at him to know he was angry at Zach's intrusion. Anger poured off him like heat from the old radiator in her room on a cold winter night. Cole and Zach used to be friends, last year when Cole first moved to Stonecreek. He'd immediately become the de facto leader of the wild crowd at the high school, the crazy and sometimes dangerous escapades from his previous school documented on social media to make him a legend his first day on campus.

In a way it was funny because Cole had first motivated her to change her image and become part of the hard-partying group of nonconformist kids. She'd been infatuated with him from the start but hadn't realized that while she was trying to get in with the bad kids, he'd desperately wanted out.

Now she wished she'd never gone down that path in the first place. Cole acted like it was so easy to walk away, but the fact that he hadn't outright told Zach and his crew to shove off told a different story. Stonecreek was a small town and once you were pigeonholed at the high school, it was difficult to undo a reputation.

"I don't know what you're talking about," she said quietly, glancing toward Zach, then inwardly groaning when Jonah, Jocelyn and Amanda crowded around the table.

"Homecoming," Zach said. "Jocelyn said you convinced your folks to let you go to the dance."

"My dad agreed," Morgan clarified. "My mom is dead."

"Whatever," Zach muttered, like he was mad she'd contradicted him.

She looked up through her lashes to see Cole glaring at Zach and then back at her, a muscle ticking in his jaw. Morgan gave a small shake of her head. The last thing she needed—that either of them needed—was Cole getting into trouble at school.

"So what's the plan?" Jonah asked, plucking an orange sliver out of Morgan's fingers. Jonah was the consummate lackey, following Zach wherever he went like a puppy would his owner. "Do we make an appearance at the dance first, then duck out or do a little prepartying to make it actually fun?"

"I think the dance will be fun," Morgan said, earning a disbelieving snort from Jocelyn.

"You're joking, right?" the cool blonde said with a sneer. "I say we preparty. Cole, can your brother hook us up?"

"Nope."

Jocelyn pouted and leaned into Cole's arm, making a sick pit open in Morgan's stomach. Jocelyn and Cole had dated—or at least hooked up—for a short time when he'd moved to town. Even though her self-named best girlfriend acted like she'd moved on, Morgan had a feeling she'd love another chance with Cole.

"Please," Jocelyn purred, rubbing herself all over Cole. He didn't seem to notice, but Morgan wanted to reach across the table and throat punch the girl. "Just a teensy-weensy bit of the good stuff."

Cole's gaze flicked to Morgan, then he shifted his arm away from Jocelyn. "I don't party anymore, Joce. You know that."

The girl's glossy mouth turned down at the corners. "Lame."

"I can hook us up," Zach told the group. "We'll make Boy Scout Cole our designated driver."

Jocelyn, Amanda and Jonah all laughed at that.

"I'm going to the dance," Cole said through clenched teeth. "Not to wherever you losers wind up for the night."

"Losers?" Zach's eyes narrowed. "That must make you King Loser, dude, because your list of exploits is longer than the rest of ours combined."

"Not anymore," Cole shot back.

"Well, then…" Zach hitched his chin toward Morgan. "You must be planning on going stag, because Morgan's with us." He reached out and trailed a finger along her sleeve. "Aren't you, sweetheart?"

"Of course she is," Jocelyn answered before Mor-

gan could. "We have a plan to get ready together."
She wiggled her eyebrows. "A ladies' preparty."

"Um…" Morgan licked her lips. "My dad agreed
to let me go to the dance. I'm not sure I can do anything else."

She met Cole's gaze and saw something that
looked like disappointment shadowed there. She
knew he expected her to take a stand against their
friends the way he had, but she didn't know if she
was strong enough for that.

Not that she wanted to be part of their stupid antics anymore. Morgan might chafe against the expectations of her grandmother, but she wasn't into
getting drunk or high every weekend. She knew she
was smart enough to be accepted at a decent college
if she tried. That was her ticket out of Stonecreek,
and she wasn't going to blow it.

"You'll find a way," Jocelyn said, undeterred.
"You always do."

"What's it going to be, Cole?" Zach arched a brow.
"You giving up your date or are you going to join us
for homecoming?"

"We really just want to go to the dance," Morgan offered quickly. "Maybe we can meet up with
you there?"

"Why does your dad have to be so strict all of a
sudden?" Jocelyn asked, her voice a high-pitched
whine. "My parents barely notice me."

Morgan shrugged. "It's annoying." She felt pres-
sured to appear that she didn't like her father taking
an interest in her life, even though the opposite was
true. Somehow she didn't think this group would appreciate the fact that she liked it.

Again, she could tell Cole didn't approve of how she was dealing with the situation. He grabbed his lunch tray and climbed off of the bench. "I need to stop by the library," he announced.

"Boy Scout," Zach muttered.

"I can go with you," Morgan offered, starting to stand.

Cole shook his head. "Stay here with your friends," he said and each word felt like a condemnation.

Then he turned and walked away.

"I liked him better before he went all try-hard," Amanda said, then popped her gum.

"He's not a try-hard," Morgan shot back. "Cole is who he is, and he doesn't care what anyone else thinks."

"Which makes him a total tool," Zach said, and Morgan could hear the irritation in his voice. Zach didn't like that Cole wouldn't run with their crew anymore. "Why did you agree to go to the dance with him anyway? If you'd wanted an official date, babe, I would have asked you."

Morgan bit her bottom lip. She couldn't admit her feelings for Cole to anyone at this table. They'd use it against her without a doubt.

"He works for Griffin Stone," she said finally. "My sister is dating him, so I knew if Griffin vouched for Cole, Maggie would help convince my dad to let me go to the dance."

All four of them stared at her like she was speaking Latin.

Then Zach let out a loud laugh. "Convoluted but also brilliant. I like that about you, Spencer. You don't look manipulative, but at the core, you're the same as the rest of us." He stood and patted the top of her head as if she were a dog.

I'm nothing like you, she wanted to scream, but kept her mouth shut. Jocelyn, Amanda and Jonah got up and followed Zach out of the cafeteria.

Morgan shoved her uneaten lunch into the paper sack and fisted one hand around it, dashing at her cheeks with the other. She wouldn't cry over those stupid jerks and the mess she'd gotten herself into trying to be friends with them.

She tossed her lunch into the trash bin, then headed for the library, making sure she didn't run into any of her fake friends on the way. Cole sat at a table directly in front of the librarian's counter.

Morgan waved to Mrs. Shamsi, the school librarian, then pulled out the chair next to Cole.

"I'm studying," he said tightly.

She leaned in and covered his open notebook with one hand. "I'm sorry."

"I'm not going to make you choose," he said, looking up at her, his eyes fierce. "There's no 'it's me or them.' That's a little too John Hughes for my taste."

She flashed a quick smile. "John Hughes was more about figuring out who you are and accepting yourself so other people will, too."

He shook his head but one side of his mouth curved. "You know what I mean, Morgan."

"I want to go to the dance with you," she promised. "I don't care about a preparty or a postparty or doing anything with Zach and Jocelyn."

"Are you going to let them in on that?"

She sighed. "It's not easy. They've been my friends for the past year, and I don't want to be rude."

"You don't want to be rude to the meanest people at this school." He lifted his hand to the back of her neck and drew her in for a quick kiss. "You're really something, Morgan Spencer."

She felt color flood her cheeks and she dipped her chin, darting a glance around the crowded library to see if anyone had noticed what he'd just done. "You kissed me," she whispered, her lips still tingling and sparks shooting down her spine.

He inclined his head. "Beautiful, smart and observant. A triple threat."

No one seemed to be paying any attention to the two of them, except Camryn Clarke, who sat at a far table in the corner with a couple other girls Morgan recognized from the science and technology program.

Camryn lived two doors down from Morgan and the two had been best friends until middle school. Once Morgan hit her teen years, it had been too difficult to spend time with Camryn at her perfect house with her perfect mother, who baked extra cookies to send home with Morgan. As if a batch of homemade cookies would make up for not having a mom. In fact, it had done the opposite. All Mrs. Clarke's kindness had accomplished was making Morgan miss her own mom more.

As Morgan started to rebel, she'd drifted apart from Camryn. *Drifted* wasn't actually the right word. She'd cut Camryn from her life, along with any other friend who reminded her of what her family had lost. It was easier to gravitate toward other misfits, kids who didn't ask her about not having a mom because they were too busy with their own dysfunction.

But now Camryn offered an approving smile and a nod toward Cole. To her surprise, Morgan found herself returning the smile.

"You're a lucky guy," she said, shifting her attention back to Cole.

"Damn right," he agreed, glancing at his watch. "A lucky guy who's going to be late for fifth period if I don't motor. You want to walk with me?"

She hesitated. "I need to grab a book from Mrs. Shamsi. I'll see you after seventh?"

He stood, then bent to kiss her again.

"The library is not the place for that, Mr. Maren."

Morgan pressed a hand to her cheek at the sound of the librarian's disapproving tone.

"Sorry," Cole told the older woman, then turned to face Morgan. *Not sorry*, he mouthed, making her smile again.

When he was gone, Morgan stood and walked toward the far end of the library. "Hey, Camryn," she said, her hands clenched in nervous fists at her sides.

"Hey, Morgan." Camryn rose from the table and picked up her backpack. "I'm heading to chemistry."

"Me, too," Morgan told her.

Camryn made a face. "I know. We're in the same class."

"Oh, right."

"Let's go."

"I was wondering if you'd want to hang out sometime," Morgan said in a rush of breath as they started down the hall. "Maybe go shopping for homecoming dresses? Maggie's going to take me this weekend. I'm sure you could come, too."

"Seriously?" The other girl looked dubious. "You want to hang out with me?"

"Sure."

"What happened to Jocelyn? She get sent to rehab already?"

Morgan snorted, then covered her mouth with one hand. "Wow," she breathed.

"I know. Sorry." Camryn adjusted the straps on her backpack. "But those girls, and the guys they run with, are bad news."

"I'm getting that," Morgan admitted.

"Cole's pretty cute, though." Camryn threw her a sidelong glance. "He stopped a couple of seniors from giving me grief in gym class because I was so bad at basketball. He's cool."

"Oh." Another layer of warmth unfurled inside Morgan. "Yeah, he's both those things."

"My mom wanted to take me dress shopping," Camryn said as they reached the classroom.

"That's fine," Morgan said quickly, sorrow stabbing at her chest. Mostly she was used to not having a mom, and Maggie did a great job of always being there for her. Even Grammy tried in her own way. But there were some times when she missed her mother even though it had been so many years that her memories had faded to fuzzy images. That lack of clarity hurt more than anything.

"She has horrible taste," Camryn continued. "I'd love to go with you and Maggie. I'll have a chance of buying a dress that doesn't make me look like I'm joining the convent or something."

Morgan took a deep breath as relief flooded

through her. "Awesome. I'll talk to Maggie and text you about the time."

"It's a plan," Camryn said with a smile. "Welcome back, Morgan."

"Thanks," Morgan said softly, understanding exactly what her old friend meant. "I'm glad to be back."

Nerves skittered across Maggie's skin as Griffin unlocked the door to their room in the quaint bed-and-breakfast at the end of a quiet street in Lychen.

"Not exactly the Four Seasons," he said with a grimace as he flipped on the light. The decor was vintage seventies with lace curtains and a four-poster bed with a flowery comforter covering it.

"I love it," Maggie said, then bit her bottom lip. How easy it would be to substitute the word *you* in that sentence. Now that she'd admitted her feelings once to Griffin, she wanted to blurt those three words every time she opened her mouth.

"You're easy to please," he said and drew her closer for a deep kiss. His hands wound around her waist, fingers edging up her tailored shirt until she felt his touch along the bare skin of her back.

"With you," she told him, "I might just be plain easy."

She felt his smile against her mouth. "You are precious to me, Maggie. You're beautiful and intelligent and you make me crazy with desire." He pulled back and his gaze held so much intensity it took her breath away. "I've never felt this way."

"I…" She paused and licked her lips. "Me neither." Somehow she couldn't bring herself to say the words

I love you again. They rested on the tip of her tongue but wouldn't spill over. What if she pushed him away by wanting more than he could give?

"Are you hungry now?" he asked, then hitched his chin toward the bed. "Or do you want a rest?"

She grabbed the hem of her shirt and pulled it over her head. "A rest," she whispered. "But I'm not tired."

"Then no rest for you," he answered with a wicked grin and covered her breast with one large hand. She gasped as the lace tickled her skin and the warmth of his touch made heat pool low in her belly. His finger traced her puckered nipple through the fabric and Maggie thought she'd never felt something so exquisite.

He gave the same attention to her other breast before moving closer. He claimed her mouth and the kiss made her crazy with need. Dropping to his knees in front of her, he reached around and unzipped the skirt she wore, then tugged it down over her hips.

Sensation swirled through her as she felt his breath at the apex of her thighs. He pulled her panties down, as well, but Maggie couldn't even feel nervous at being exposed to him in this way. All she could feel was desire building, and when he dipped a finger into her, she gave a yearning moan.

"So beautiful," he murmured, pushing gently on her legs, encouraging her to open more for him.

She happily gave him all the access he wanted, running her fingers through his hair as his tongue found her most sensitive spot.

"Griffin." She said his name in a hoarse breath, but he didn't pause as he lavished attention on her. She was outside her body, floating on a mounting wave of blissful pressure. Then the wave crashed over her, sending her exploding up and then spiraling back down as her whole body hummed with the electric release. Her knees gave way and she would have sank to the carpet, but Griffin was there to catch her. He looped his arms behind her knees and back to carry her to the bed.

He threw back the covers and put her down on the mattress, then efficiently shucked out of his clothes. He pulled a wallet from the pocket of his jeans and took out a condom wrapper. Maggie watched, mesmerized by the muscles that bunched with every movement and overwhelmed that this man was here with her.

Then he was on the bed, adjusting himself between her thighs. "Are you good?"

She nodded and reached up to push away the hair that fell over his forehead. "I think I'm about to be great," she said, then gasped as he filled her.

They moved together, a tangle of arms and legs, and Maggie was hard-pressed to know where she left off and he began. She could barely catch her breath in a maelstrom of kissing, touching and a rhythm that was singular to the two of them. Her muscles tensed as if anticipating the pleasure to come.

Then she was breaking apart again and only remained tethered to reality by the way Griffin whispered her name as he found his own release.

He held her close as her breathing returned to normal, and she could feel his heart pounding in his chest.

When he lifted his head to gaze at her, she smiled. "I

have a better appreciation for the 'Afternoon Delight' song."

He chuckled and kissed the tip of her nose. "There were definitely some skyrockets going off just then."

When he headed to the bathroom, Maggie pulled the sheet and comforter up to her chest. Her limbs felt like jelly, warm, pliant and totally satisfied. She could stay like this forever, she thought as her eyes drifted closed.

"Sleepy now?" Griffin asked as he climbed under the sheets and pulled her close so her back was snuggled against the warmth of his chest, the short hair there tickling her bare skin.

"Nope," she said around a yawn. "Okay, maybe."

"We have time for a nap," he told her.

"But I don't want to miss any part of this day," she said, even though it was a struggle to form a coherent sentence.

"We have all the time in the world," he promised and she drifted to sleep with a smile on her face and her heart full.

Chapter Thirteen

Griffin let himself into the room three hours later to find Maggie propped up against a pillow in the bed, wearing one of the B and B's white bathrobes.

Her hair fell in damp waves over her shoulders, so different from the polished style she usually wore. It reminded him of their night at the cabin in the woods, when she'd fallen out of the canoe and ended up soaked and sputtering.

The memory made him smile. Although things had gone horribly wrong the next morning when he'd found out the tasting room had been damaged in a fire accidentally set by Maggie's sister, it had also been the night Griffin realized he was falling in love with her.

"I woke up and you were gone. What's wrong?" she asked, inclining her head as she used the remote to mute the TV.

"Nothing." He forced a smile.

I'm in love with you, he thought silently.

Why did it terrify him so much? She'd said the words to him, so all he had to do now was reciprocate. Maggie was an amazing woman. Any man would be lucky to have her.

"I brought food, clothing and wine," he said, trying to shove down the fear that clogged his throat. He should be happy. People fell in love every day. But Griffin had never allowed himself to get that close to anyone, to open himself up to being rejected the way his father had done.

"You're like a Maslow's hierarchy of needs fulfiller." She straightened from the bed and padded toward him, reaching for the bags.

"What kind of food and what kind of clothes? I'm assuming I don't need to ask about the wine."

"Carryout from Luigi's. I hope you don't mind I didn't try something new on this visit." Luigi's Italian Inn was the restaurant where they'd had dinner their first time in Lychen. Griffin knew Maggie loved the savory northern Italian dishes and wanted to recreate everything that was good about their first date.

"I'm so hungry," Maggie told him by way of an answer. "This is perfect."

"I also have a Kiss Me I'm from Oregon T-shirt and a pair of Oregon Ducks sweatpants for you." He wiggled his eyebrows. "No undies in the gift shop around the corner, so you're going commando for the night, Ms. Spencer."

She giggled at that and gave him a saucy grin. "To be honest, I wasn't planning to spend much time dressed, so that should work out just fine."

"Killing me," he murmured and leaned in to kiss her.

"I take that as a compliment," she answered, peering into the bag with the food. "Shall we eat?"

He glanced around the room. "I forgot about a wine opener. Why don't you set up dinner and I'll borrow one from the front desk?"

She nodded and he dropped the bag of clothes to the floor, handed Maggie the bottle of wine, then let himself out of the room.

In the hallway, he bent forward, hands on knees, and drew in several deep breaths. Should he tell her he loved her? Was it real? Before Maggie he hadn't even thought he was capable of love. He'd had his share of relationships, and Cassie had been a good friend since they'd realized they were too alike to actually be a good match, but he'd always found a way to end things with the women he'd dated before they got too serious. It was easier that way, he'd told himself.

Griffin knew what it was like to love someone with your whole heart and not have those feelings reciprocated. It embarrassed him that his dysfunctional relationship with his dad had left him so deeply scarred, but that was the truth of it. And it was why he'd always kept his emotions so closely guarded.

Maggie had managed to work her way through every layer of his defenses until she filled a place in his soul he hadn't even known was empty.

He stood and moved toward the staircase, running a hand through his hair. He could make this work. She was worth making this work. Now he saw that his reaction to the fire and her sister's involvement had been a defense mechanism, an excuse to push her away because she'd been getting too close.

What a damn coward he was.

No more.

He retrieved a wine opener and took the steps to the second floor two at a time. Maggie whirled around and clasped a hand to her chest as he burst into the room.

"You scared me," she said with a breathy laugh. "You must be even hungrier than I am."

"I love you," he blurted.

Her mouth fell open, then snapped shut. She stared at him, as if trying to process his declaration.

"Sorry," he murmured. "I didn't mean to shock you."

She frowned. "Sorry you love me?"

"Not for a minute," he answered. "Falling in love with you is the smartest thing I've done in ages, even if it wasn't on purpose."

She huffed out a laugh and placed the napkins she held on the table. "You didn't want to fall in love?" She moved toward him.

"I didn't plan on it."

"Me neither," she admitted softly, placing her hands on his shoulders.

"But…"

"I love you so much," she whispered, and the happiness that rocketed through him almost drove him to his knees with its power.

He bent his head and brushed his lips over hers, and it felt like kissing her for the first time. "I love you," he said against her mouth.

"I wasn't sure," she admitted, "I was afraid I'd ruined things by saying it too soon."

"Never be afraid to tell me how you feel." He tucked her hair behind her ears, dropping kisses on her nose and then on each of her eyelids. He wanted to kiss her everywhere, to lay her out and worship every beautiful inch of her.

Then her stomach growled.

"Priorities," he said with a grin.

"Yeah," she agreed, making a face. "I wasn't joking when I said I was hungry."

He stepped back and pulled the corkscrew from where he'd stashed it in his back pocket. "Then let's eat and drink."

"Should I put on my new outfit first?" Maggie asked, eyeing the bag of clothes.

"I'd prefer if you didn't," he answered. "It will only mean I have to undress you again after dinner."

"The robe is so comfy." She turned to the small table where she'd set out the cartons of food and the paper plates the restaurant had given him.

"What were you watching?" he asked as he uncorked the wine.

"HGTV. It's my favorite thing."

He laughed. "You like remodeling shows? If I'd known, I would have put you to work on the tasting room."

"I like watching," she clarified. "Not necessarily doing." She glanced at the television. "Lucas and Megan from *Fix My Flip* are my favorites. He's the contractor and she does interior design. They help people with horror-story flipped houses make them better. At first they were just business partners but got engaged in the season finale. It's so romantic."

"That's a thing?" he asked, shaking his head. "Not much about construction is romantic in my experience."

"Have you ever gotten busy with a girl in one of your unfinished projects?"

The wine cork popped out at that moment and Griffin almost dropped the bottle onto the floor. "Um...no," he said with a laugh.

She dished out portions of chicken parmesan and Caesar salad to each of them. "What about in the rows of grapes?"

"Maggie Spencer," he said with mock shock, "do you have some sort of sex-in-public-places fantasy?"

"Maybe," she said, winking.

"Eat fast," he told her, pouring the wine. "Just imagining you naked in the vineyard is driving me wild."

"Good to know," she told him. "I'm thinking of an early Christmas present involving a bow and a trench coat."

"Already the best gift ever," he murmured, making her laugh once again.

He loved the sound of her laughter and the fact that he was the one who made her happy. He unmuted the TV so they could watch *Fix My Flip* while they ate.

There truly were no words to describe the perfection of this getaway. It was more than the physical connection they shared. Sitting in a hotel room watching some random remodeling show with Maggie was more exciting than anything he'd done in years. He had a close set of buddies from the army and other friends he'd made during his career in construction. Griffin had watched many of them get married over the years, several times as a groomsman at the front of the church.

He'd never understood the desire to bind himself to one person for his entire life before Maggie. The daily grind of marriage had seemed like a cage from where he'd stood ruthlessly guarding his freedom. He'd thought that being uncommitted made things better, but now he couldn't imagine going back to being alone.

Not when he could spend his nights with Maggie.

This was what he wanted, so much that it made his chest burn with yearning.

"Shiplap," she said between bites, nodding toward the television. "I looove shiplap."

Griffin felt his brow furrow as he watched the renovation show hosts nailing rough-sawed boards to the walls. "You say that like other women talk about diamonds or fancy shoes."

"Fancy shoes hurt my feet," she answered. "But shiplap makes me happy." She took a sip of wine. "I'm going to hire someone to install it when I move back into my house next year."

At his snort, she frowned. "Okay, fine. I'll learn to do it myself. No judgment from you."

"Your boyfriend," he said, hitching a thumb at his chest, "just happens to be an experienced contractor. I can put up shiplap or teach you how to do it yourself if you want."

"Oh." Pink colored her cheeks as she took another long drink of wine. "You're my boyfriend?"

"I just told you I love you," he explained. "I think we can safely say I'm your boyfriend."

She stared at him for a moment, then nodded. "I like the sound of that."

"Have you ever—" he leaned across the table, dropping his voice to a low whisper "—had sex on a table saw?"

Her loud cackle of laughter filled the room. "Eww...splinters."

He grinned, once again so easily charmed by her.

"I'll wipe it down first," he promised, and she laughed again. "Right. That doesn't sound much better."

"Shh." Maggie lifted a finger to her lips. "Don't talk, darling. Just sit there and look pretty."

He pushed back from the table. "Now you're poking the bear."

Her eyes widened. "Nope."

"Oh, yes," he said, moving toward her.

She shifted her chair to face him and loosened the sash on her robe. The soft fabric parted until he could almost see her breasts. God, he wanted to see her breasts.

"I hope you've had enough to eat," he said, taking her hand and pulling her to standing. "Because I need to get you back into that bed more than I need my next breath."

She undid the sash completely and opened the robe until it fell from her shoulders, a small smile playing on her gorgeous mouth. "What are you waiting for?"

Needing no further encouragement, Griffin wrapped his arms around her.

The following Saturday, Maggie drove Morgan and her friend Camryn to Portland for dress shopping. They stopped for lunch at a popular Mexican restaurant first, the two girls pulling up various photos of homecoming dress options while they ate.

Maggie couldn't remember the last time she'd seen her sister seem truly happy hanging out with a friend.

Whenever Jocelyn or anyone from that group had come to the house, there'd been sneering and sassy comebacks if the girls had been forced to interact with the family.

Today Morgan seemed more like her old self, the girl she'd been before deciding to be a wild child. They started at one of Maggie's favorite stores, Sweet Threads, where both girls tried on at least a dozen dresses each.

Maggie played the part of chaperone, steering them toward styles with which neither Grammy nor Camryn's conservative mother could find fault.

Morgan chose an open-backed, floral-print dress in shades of blue, which made her look like a fairy-tale princess, while Camryn settled on a dark pink two-piece A-line that highlighted her dark hair and olive complexion. They got shoes to match at a different boutique and Maggie bought a pair of earrings for each of them.

"What about you?" Morgan asked Maggie as the girls loaded their purchases into the back of her Volkswagen.

Maggie waved her hand, brushing aside the question. "This trip isn't about me."

"But you have the reunion dance," Morgan insisted.

"Oh, yeah," Camryn chimed in. "The old people event."

"Not quite old," Maggie objected with a smile.

The two teenagers shared a look, which Maggie chose to ignore.

"Come on, Mags." Morgan shut the trunk and tugged on Maggie's wrist. "I totally forgot about you when I was trying on dresses, but now we can focus on your dance."

Spoken like a true teenager.

"I didn't see anything I wanted for myself," Maggie lied. She'd planned to shop for a new dress but felt silly after listening to the girls discuss styles most of the morning. She wasn't a kid and the reunion dance shouldn't mean that much to her.

Except it did.

The dance would be her and Griffin's first outing as a true couple. Yes, they'd gone on dates and made tongues wag at the hospital gala, but it felt like things had changed since their night away on the coast. Attending the reunion dance together would solidify their relationship to everyone in town. There'd be no more flying under the radar after that. Maggie was ready, and she had to believe Griffin was, as well.

He'd told her he loved her and called himself her boyfriend.

They'd talked about plans for her house once her tenants' lease was up, and Griffin had seemed totally invested in helping her with her renovation projects.

That meant he was planning to stay in Stonecreek, didn't it? She mentally chided herself for not having the nerve to ask him outright. But she hadn't wanted to spoil the mood of the evening.

So she'd avoided any topics that would have caused either of them stress. Thank God for her love of remodeling shows because it would have been a pretty quiet night without that.

Griffin hadn't seemed to notice the big ole elephant in the room. He'd been loving and attentive— so attentive her toes curled remembering all the ways he'd brought her pleasure. But he had no apparent issues with avoiding difficult subjects.

That couldn't last forever, obviously, although she'd been so busy in the past week with campaign functions and the start of planning the winter carnival that she'd only managed to carve out one night with him. Because of their respective living situations, the date had ended with a hot and heavy make-out session in the Land Cruiser's back seat.

Another thing from her teenage bucket list that Maggie was finally checking off in her late twenties.

"Come on," Morgan coaxed. "That second store we went to—the one with the snobby saleslady—had some matronly dresses you'd love."

Maggie sniffed. "I don't love matronly dresses."

Morgan and Camryn shared another look.

"Then pick something for me if you think you can do better."

"We thought you'd never ask," Camryn said with a smile.

Morgan looped an arm around Maggie's waist. "Griffin isn't going to know what hit him at that reunion dance."

"I doubt that's true," Maggie said but secretly cheered as the girls led her back down the street. They insisted she try on a dizzying array of dresses, but she finally settled on a wine-colored high-low gown in a gorgeous chiffon fabric.

"It might be too much," she told Morgan even as the saleswoman—who was far friendlier when it became clear Maggie was a guaranteed sale—wrapped up the purchase.

"It's perfect," Morgan assured her as Camryn

stepped away to take a call from her mother. "I bet Mom would have loved it."

Sudden tears pricked the backs of Maggie's eyes. "I know she's watching over us," she whispered. "She'd be so proud of you, Mo-Mo."

"Then she had low expectations," Morgan said, shaking her head. "But I'm working on getting better."

"You're doing a great job, sweetie. In the end, each of us is a work in progress."

Morgan laughed. "Now you sound like Dad and his armchair philosophy nuggets."

"He's better at it."

"You do okay," Morgan said, nudging Maggie's arm.

They stopped for ice cream, then drove back to Stonecreek, dropping off Camryn before heading home. Grammy's car sat parked outside the house, eliciting a groan from Morgan.

"What a way to end the day," the girl muttered.

"We don't know why she's here," Maggie cautioned. "It could just be a friendly, grandmotherly visit."

"You keep telling yourself that."

Maggie had to admit she couldn't remember the last time her grandmother had stopped by without an agenda.

After hanging both dresses in the front closet and leaving the other shopping bags at the foot of the stairs, she found her father and Grammy sitting at the kitchen table, a photo album open between them.

"Hey, girls," Dad called when she and Morgan walked in. "Successful shopping trip?"

Morgan nodded. "It was awesome. I got this totally fantastic blue flowery dress and helped Maggie pick out one for the reunion dance. I love Portland. It's the best city."

Jim looked dumbfounded at his younger daughter's enthusiastic reply and even more so when Morgan walked to the table and gave him a quick hug, then bent to kiss Grammy's cheek.

"You need a haircut," Grammy said, tugging at the ends of Morgan's long locks.

Maggie inwardly winced but Morgan only smiled. "One step ahead of you, Grammy. I have an appointment Wednesday after school. Want to drive me?"

Vivian's eyes widened slightly but she gave a quick nod. "I'd love to. I'll pick you up at the high school. We could visit the bakery when you're finished at the salon. Marionberry is the pie flavor of the month."

"That's my favorite," Morgan told her.

Grammy patted her arm. "Yes, dear. I know."

"It's a date, then." Morgan glanced at the clock that hung on the wall next to the refrigerator. "I have homework to finish."

Their father nodded. "Ben is at Aidan's house. He's supposed to be back by six, so we'll eat then."

"Sounds good." Morgan gave Maggie another hug and a whispered thank-you, then headed upstairs.

"That must have been some shopping trip," Jim said when she'd left the room. "I haven't seen her that happy in years."

"She's excited about the dance," Maggie said, but she hoped it was more than that. She wanted to believe Morgan was truly working through her teenage demons to become the amazing young woman Maggie knew she had the potential to be.

"You found a dress, as well?" Grammy asked, lifting an eyebrow.

"It's very pretty," Maggie told her, not giving any more details. Of course she hoped her grandmother would like the dress, but at the same time had no desire to solicit her opinion.

"I assume Griffin is your date?"

Maggie took a breath, then said, "He's my boyfriend."

"Things have gotten serious with the two of you?" her dad asked.

Her first instinct was to offer a denial. It felt too new and precious to share, but she was sick of playing it safe. That had gotten her nowhere anyway. "I'm in love with him," she said in a rush of air.

Her father leaned back in his chair and whistled under his breath. Grammy only nodded. "He came to see me earlier today."

"What?" Maggie blurted. "Griffin?"

Vivian tapped a finger on the table. "He wanted to get my thoughts on the announcement about Harvest expanding."

Maggie frowned. He hadn't mentioned any plan to speak to her grandmother.

"He assured me that Trevor had released the plan prematurely and that the family will work with business owners in town before deciding how to proceed."

"Good," Maggie said, trying not to fidget under her grandmother's shrewd gaze. "That's the same thing I told you last week after talking to Jana."

"I believe it was a sign of respect," Vivian explained, "that Griffin came to me. He also mentioned his relationship with you."

Maggie edged closer, keeping her face neutral.

"His intentions are honorable," Grammy said with a nod. "Your involvement with one brother and now the other is unorthodox," she continued, making Maggie flinch, "but I approve of you and Griffin as a couple."

"Mom," Jim said, exasperation clear in his tone, "Maggie doesn't need anyone's approval."

Grammy sniffed. "I'm giving it just the same."

"Thank you," Maggie whispered, not quite sure how she felt about her grandmother's support in this case. Her father was right. She didn't need her family to sanction her relationship. But the truth was she didn't want to be at odds with her grandmother. Despite Vivian's tendency toward judgment and manipulation, Maggie loved her dearly.

"I brought over the album because I wanted you to see this photo of your mother." She touched her finger to the edge of one of the old photos. It showed Nancy Spencer holding Maggie as a baby, so she must have been in her early twenties at the time.

"It was her birthday," Jim murmured, his tone wistful.

"I gave her the necklace she was wearing as a gift," Vivian explained. "My mother had given it to me when I turned eighteen. It was the year I met your grandfather. Her mother had worn it on the boat over from Ireland. It's a family heirloom."

Maggie bent forward and peered at the amber stone set in gold. "It's beautiful. She looks so happy."

Her father nodded. "Being a mother made her happy. You, Morgan and Ben were her life."

Maggie glanced up sharply at him. "You were part of it, too. Mom loved being your wife as much as she did our mother."

His gaze took on a troubled cast but he smiled at her.

"I found this as I was clearing out my dresser," Grammy continued, pulling a small black box from her purse. "I'm not sure how I ended up with it again."

Maggie's dad blew out a long breath. "It was when I got rid of all of her belongings as part of my grieving process." He rubbed a hand over his eyes. "The anger stage, which lasted way too long in my case. You saved some things for the girls."

Sorrow pinched Maggie's chest at the thought of all the physical mementos she'd never have, and her grandmother's mouth thinned. "I remember now. Anyway, I have the necklace and I thought you might want to wear it to the reunion dance." She opened the box, revealing the delicate piece of jewelry on a cushion of black velvet. "I wore it to my senior prom."

Maggie drew in a shaky breath.

"If it's not to your taste, then you can simply keep it with your other jewelry," Grammy said in a clipped tone, obviously misinterpreting Maggie's silence.

"I'd be honored to wear it to the dance," Maggie told her. She plucked up the gold chain to examine it more closely. "I feel like I remember Mom wearing the necklace, although I suppose it could be just from seeing the photos."

"Your mom loved it," her dad said gently. "She wore it for every special occasion."

"You ordered two sodas, sir," the waiter said, condemnation dripping from his tone.

Jonah snickered.

His face flushing bright pink, Cole pulled out his wallet and threw a twenty on the table. "For your trouble," he muttered.

"Big spender," Zach said, standing and nudging Cole.

"Shut up," Cole told him.

When they were all out on the sidewalk, Zach slung an arm over Cole's shoulders. "Don't be mad, bro. I save you loads of money back there. Hell, you could buy us all dinner at The Kitchen and still get off cheaper than the Grille would have cost you."

Cole kept his gaze straight ahead as he led them down the street toward the diner. "Whatever."

"I'm so glad we're all together." Jocelyn took Morgan's hand. "It's exactly how I planned tonight to go."

Unfortunately, Morgan's plan for a romantic night with Cole had been ruined in the process. He wouldn't even make eye contact with her and sat at the far end of the table during dinner. Did he really think she'd planned this? Or that she wanted to be with Jocelyn and her group?

Zach insisted that he and Jocelyn pile into Cole's truck while Jonah and Amanda follow, preventing Morgan from getting any moment in private with Cole to explain that she was as unhappy about the turn of events as he was.

The parking lot at the high school was almost full by the time they arrived, with underclassmen being dropped off by parents.

As Cole turned off the car, Zach pulled a vape

pen from the inside pocket of his jacket. "Quick hit before we head into la-la land?"

"You can't do that in here," Cole said through clenched teeth.

"Boy Scout," Zach muttered under his breath as he climbed out. As soon as the door shut, Zach took a quick hit. The others joined him while Cole remained on the other side of the vehicle, arms crossed tightly over his chest.

"I'm sorry," Morgan said as she approached him, wanting to be as far away from the illegal activity as possible.

"It's fine."

"They recognized your truck, then saw us in the window. I didn't tell them anything."

He shot her a doubtful glance. "I don't care either way."

"I do," she said, anger swelling inside her. "I was having a great time with you, and they ruined it. I hate that you think I wanted this."

His silence hurt her more than any words could have.

"Be that way. I'm here to go to the dance, not to stand out in the parking lot with them." She started forward toward the high school's main entrance.

Cole was at her side a moment later, lacing his fingers with hers. "I'm sorry, too," he whispered.

She dashed a tear from the corner of one eye, then flashed a smile. "It's not your fault."

"Morgan, I want you to know—"

"Wait up, lovebirds."

Suddenly they were surrounded again, Cole letting go of her hand when Zach tried to jump on his back.

"Knock it off," he shouted.

"Maybe you'll get crowned king of the home-coming party poopers," Amanda said, giggling obnoxiously at her own joke.

Then they were in the dance, the thumping music and lights from the DJ's table overwhelming.

Morgan pulled in a sharp breath. This had been such a mistake. She would have been better off skipping the whole thing.

"Do you want to dance?" Cole asked, eyeing the crowd jumping up and down in unison in front of them.

"Not yet," she admitted. "That looks a little intense for me."

"Jonah has a flask," Jocelyn said, leaning in to whisper in Morgan's ear.

"I'm not drinking tonight," Morgan told her.

Jocelyn groaned and put her hand to her forehead, making an L shape with her thumb and forefinger.

"She's here." Amanda rushed up to them, grabbing onto Jocelyn's arms. "On the other side of the gym by the bleachers."

"Not now," Jocelyn said on a hiss of breath.

Morgan looked to the far end of the gym and saw Camryn standing with a group of girls. She knew her friend was going to the dance with friends instead of a date, and a sliver of unease snaked its way along her spine at the thought of Jocelyn or Amanda singling out any of those girls.

Before she could ask about it, the music changed to a slow ballad. Cole tugged her hand.

"Now's our chance." He gently pulled her toward the dance floor and all Morgan could do was glance back over her shoulder at the two mean girls. They were intently watching something on Amanda's phone, so Morgan figured she was safe to ignore them for at least a few minutes.

It felt super good to be dancing with Cole, even if she was distracted. "Way better," he said, his warm hands resting on her back.

"Mmm-hmm." She shuffled her feet to get a better view of Jocelyn and Amanda.

"I'm still glad we came tonight, even if the loser crew almost ruined it."

Several couples had joined them on the dance floor, blocking Morgan's view.

"Are you happy?"

"No," she breathed, craning her neck.

"I knew it. This was a mistake. I told you I was no good for you. If you'd gone with a boy who—"

"No," Morgan shouted, whirling out of Cole's arms. She'd caught sight of Jocelyn and Amanda pulling bags of what looked like flour from their purses, like they were replaying a scene from *Carrie* or that Drew Barrymore movie where the mean boys tried to dump dog food on Leelee Sobieski at the dance.

She pushed her way through the crowd. "Camryn, move," she yelled to her friend, who glanced over, confusion in her gentle eyes.

"Shut up, Spencer," she heard Zach call from the edge of the dance floor.

"Go," she called, and Camryn took several quick steps away from the bleachers just as white powder sprayed across the floor.

"You ruined it," Jocelyn screeched, moving out

of the shadows and toward Morgan. "Our plan was perfect."

"Not my plan," Morgan clarified loudly. "And there's nothing perfect about deliberate cruelty. Find another way to amuse yourself besides bullying people, Jocelyn. I'm done with your high and mighty attitude, and I bet I'm not the only one."

A few girls standing near the edge of the dance floor clapped.

One side of Jocelyn's brightly painted mouth curled into a sneer. "Shut up, you stupid bi—"

"Enough." Cole stepped forward, placing a hand on Morgan's back. "Most of us are here to have a good time." He pointed toward Jocelyn, then turned his gaze to Zach. "If you people can't deal with that, you should leave."

"Great idea, Cole." Dr. Cuthbert, the school's stout principal, appeared behind Zach. "Zach and Jocelyn, your time at the homecoming dance is officially done."

"It sucked anyway," Zach muttered. "Come on, guys."

Jocelyn continued to glare at Morgan. "You're going to regret this."

Morgan shook her head. "I doubt that."

With another angry huff, Jocelyn turned and stalked after Zach. Amanda and Jonah followed close on their heels.

While Dr. Cuthbert called for someone to clean up the mess in front of the bleachers, Camryn approached Morgan.

"I'm sorry they were such jerks," Morgan said

softly, hating that she'd ever had any association with that group.

"You saved me," Camryn told her.

"I just stopped them from doing something really mean and stupid."

Camryn smiled. "Which happened to save me. Thanks." She hugged Morgan, then was called away by another friend.

Morgan could feel people staring at her and refused to make eye contact with any of them.

"You okay?" Cole asked, shifting closer.

"Can we get out of here?"

Without hesitation he took her hand and led her from the overheated gymnasium. Once outside, she drew in a deep breath of the cool fall air. The night was clear and stars littered the night sky, but Morgan had trouble appreciating the beauty of it.

"That was the worst homecoming dance in the history of the world." She wiped at her eyes, embarrassed when tears flowed down her cheeks. This night was supposed to be perfect and now it had been ruined from start to finish.

"Not for me," Cole said softly.

He shrugged out of his jacket and draped it over her shoulders when she shivered.

"You're done with Jocelyn," he clarified.

"Very done," she confirmed.

"Then everything is great—better than great." He drew his thumb along her cheek. "Although I'm sorry you're upset."

She sighed. "I'm mainly upset that I didn't see them for the jerks they were from the start."

"We all make mistakes." He laced their fingers together. "Trust me, I'm the poster child for mistakes."

"Are you going to take me home now?"

"No way. We've got a couple more hours until your dad expects you back, right?"

She pulled her phone from her purse and checked the time. "Yeah." Suddenly nerves skittered across her skin. Cole's gaze on her was dark and unreadable. Four months ago she'd done a really bad job of trying to seduce him but now...

How was she supposed to tell him she wasn't ready for that? She liked him so much—in fact, she was pretty sure she was falling in love with him. But that didn't mean...

"How about ice cream?"

Her gaze flicked to his. "Ice cream?"

"And a hamburger." He rubbed his stomach. "I barely ate anything earlier and I noticed you didn't, either."

"Being with Zach and them made me lose my appetite."

"Me, too." His grin was kind of goofy and totally endearing. "But now I'm starving."

"Food sounds great."

They walked to his truck and he unlocked the door and opened it for her. Before she could climb in, he turned and cupped her face in his hands. "You were amazing tonight," he whispered and then his lips grazed hers.

Heat spiraled through her as she wound her arms around his neck. It didn't matter that she was only sixteen. Morgan knew this kiss and this boy would ruin her for whatever might follow. The kiss broke her apart, then put her back together, but different, because how could she be anything else when he turned her whole world upside down?

This moment was amazing and made everything worth it. Cole was worth it. Finally Morgan realized she was, too. She thought about Maggie's words from last weekend and was happy to know that she'd finally given her mom a reason to be proud.

Maggie checked her appearance in the hallway mirror one more time, fingering the amber necklace she wore, then glancing at the clock above the mantel. Griffin was almost twenty minutes late. An uneasy feeling had settled over her and no matter how many times she tried to reassure herself about his feelings for her, she couldn't shake her anxiety.

The house was quiet thanks to her dad, who'd taken Morgan and Ben out to dinner so it wouldn't be quite such a throwback-to-high-school scene when Griffin came to get her.

Suddenly her phone chirped, vibrating almost insistently on the entry table. She rushed toward it, trying to tell herself that the panic welling inside her was just her mind playing tricks.

Her whole body went numb as she read the message.

Emergency in Seattle with Cassie. On the road now. Sorry about tonight.

Three simple sentences but they ripped through Maggie with the force of machine-gun fire. She was being stood up.

She smoothed a hand over her chiffon dress as

humiliation washed over her. What could be so urgent that he couldn't wait a few hours to start the drive north? Maggie wanted to give him the benefit of the doubt, but all her insecurities tumbled forward like the text had unlocked the Pandora's box that held each of her demons and set them free to wreak havoc on her heart.

A knock at the front door had her heart hammering in her chest. Maybe he'd changed his mind and turned around to be with her before rushing off to his another woman's side.

Drawing in a deep breath, she opened the door to find Trevor standing on the other side. He straightened his tie and gave her a lopsided smile, looking almost as uncomfortable as he had when she'd found him with another woman on their wedding day.

"What happened?" she demanded, knowing he must be there on Griffin's behest.

He shrugged. "I'm sorry, Mags. I don't know. He got a phone call and freaked out, throwing clothes into a bag and heading for his car without much of an explanation. It involves—"

"Cassie," she interrupted. "He texted that much."

"He shouted at me to check on you as he was walking out the door. I didn't have a chance to ask him anything more. Mom tried calling, but he's not answering."

"I'm fine."

"You're a horrible liar," Trevor said gently. Griffin had told her something similar and she vowed at that moment to figure out how not to show her emotions on her face. She was sick to death of people being able to read her every feeling, especially when it felt like she was regularly getting kicked in the gut.

"At least tell me this wasn't some grand plan hatched by the two of you to pay me back for walking away from the wedding."

He shook his head. "I'll admit it's still difficult for me to see you with my brother. One moment I'm okay with it because I know I couldn't have made you happy, but the next it grates under my skin because…" He huffed out a humorless laugh. "Basically, Griffin's getting everything I ever thought I wanted and he doesn't even seem to care."

"Trevor."

"This isn't about me." He waved a hand, dismissing her concern. "And it has nothing to do with the wedding. I promise you, Maggie."

She nodded but looked away, embarrassed anew by the tears that filled her eyes. Her life felt utterly ridiculous that after being betrayed by one brother, she'd been consoled by the other. Now the roles were reversed, only Trevor was little comfort against the yawning ache stretching across her heart.

"He cares about you," Trevor offered with a sigh. "If that helps at all."

She swallowed. "He told me he loved me." What a strange admission to make to her ex-fiancé, but she couldn't stop the words. "I believed him."

"I doubt he was lying, although I'm also not sure Griffin actually knows how to properly love someone. As fantastic as our mom is, both of us seem to take after Dad as far as our stunted emotions go."

"Not helping," she muttered.

"I wish I knew how to help." He shoved his hands

into his pockets. "If you still want to go to the dance, I could be your date. As friends, of course," he added when she looked at him sharply.

"Wouldn't the gossips in town love that?" She shook her head. "Thank you for the offer, but I couldn't hold it together at the dance. As soon as someone asks about Griffin—"

"Which would be five seconds after you got there," Trevor confirmed.

"Right? I'd lose it, and I'm done with my private life being fodder for the rumor mill around here."

"You can hold your head high, Mags." Trevor lifted a hand, like he might reach out to her, then shoved it back into his pocket. "You've done nothing wrong."

She pressed her lips together and nodded. "Too bad that doesn't make me feel any better right now."

"I hope it will soon, and I'm sure Griffin will call you once whatever he's rushing toward settles down."

"No."

Trevor's brows lifted. "He'll call, Maggie."

"I'm not sure I want to talk to him."

"You can't mean that."

"Yes," she said with more confidence than she felt, "I can. I don't know what happened to send him rushing to Seattle. But if I'm not important enough to share something like that, it isn't working. I'm not going to settle. I've done too much of that in my life. If he won't let me in on everything, I don't want anything."

"Is that what you want me to tell him?"

She met his gaze. "Out of respect for me, I'd ask

that you let me handle it. I need time to focus on the election next week."

"You're going to win," Trevor promised, and Maggie appreciated his confidence. "I won't say a word to Griffin. Do you want to know the details of why he left when we get them?"

Her stomach burned. "I don't. If it ends, I have to make a clean break. There's no other way."

"I'm sorry," he repeated and leaned in to give her a quick hug.

"Thanks for coming here. I know it wasn't easy."

"Anything for you, Mags." With a wave, he headed back to his car.

Maggie closed the door to the house, an odd calm settling over her. Her heart might be shattered into a million pieces, but she'd recover. Or at least she'd move forward past the heartbreak.

What other choice did she have? She went upstairs and took off her clothes, hanging the beautiful dress she'd bought for the dance in the back of her childhood closet. She kept the necklace on as she showered and washed off the makeup she'd so carefully applied.

Her family returned home, each of them shocked and supportive at the sudden turn of events. Her father got out ice-cream sundae supplies and they gathered around the kitchen table, each trying to comfort Maggie in their own individual ways.

"Seriously," Ben said, pumping his fist in the air, "why won't anyone let me shank one of the Stones?"

"Because you'd go to jail and I'd be sad," Maggie answered calmly.

"Yeah, Ben, who'd fart at the dinner table if you

weren't around?" Morgan asked with a smirk. "We'd miss it so much."

"No one farts at the dinner table," their father said, followed quickly by a loud trumpeting sound coming from Ben.

"We're not having dinner now," the boy said, taking an extra dollop of whipped cream. "It doesn't count."

"Are you sure you're okay?" Morgan asked, biting down on her bottom lip.

"I'll be fine," Maggie said and forced a smile. "Life happens but we keep moving on, right?"

Jim nodded. "You're the strongest person I know, Mags."

"Thanks, Dad." Maggie cleared her throat. "I think to help make me feel better that everyone should watch a movie of my choice tonight without complaining."

Both Morgan and Ben groaned. "Not the Hallmark channel again," Ben said in a whine.

Maggie shook her head. "I was thinking that disaster movie you were telling me about last week."

"Seriously?" Morgan asked. "You want to watch *Meteor Wave*? It's supposed to be terrible and so inappropriate."

"Sounds perfect," Maggie told her.

They all piled into the cozy family room and, indeed, the movie was as bad and as perfect for her mood as Maggie expected.

And when her phone hadn't rung by the time she went to bed, Maggie knew she'd made the right choice. If Griffin wanted her to be a real part of his life, he would have called. He would have shared with her whatever trouble he was having. That was what people in relationships did. Right?

But what had they really had other than a few special moments and a couple of idyllic nights together? Maggie wanted something real, something she could count on. She deserved that.

Or maybe love just wasn't in the cards for her. That was fine, too. She had a full life, family and friends she cared about and a job she loved. That would have to be enough.

At least for now.

Epilogue

"Congratulations, Maggie."

Maggie turned from Irma Cole and Chuck O'Malley to where Jana Stone stood with a mix of hope and regret in her eyes.

"Thank you."

"Is it okay that I stopped by your victory party?" the older woman asked, fidgeting with one of the buttons on her blouse. "I understand why you might not want anyone from my family here so—"

"I'm glad you came," Maggie said honestly, giving Jana a hug. "Your support during the campaign meant a lot to me."

"I know you'll do a great job for the town, like you always have. You're a good girl, Maggie."

"Hopefully Jason will get over his loss quickly."

Jana waved away that concern. "He'll find something else to complain about soon enough. That branch of the family is a bunch of negative Nellies."

Maggie smiled at the description. "Please have a drink or a piece of cake," she offered, hating the awkwardness that enveloped them.

"Griffin called a few days ago," Jana blurted.

Pain lanced through Maggie at the mention of his name, but she kept her features even. She'd become an expert at masking her emotions in the past week.

"I don't want to hear about it," she said, taking a step away.

"He had a good reason for—"

Maggie held up a hand. "I can't do this, Jana. Not tonight." She glanced around the crowded reception room at the Miriam Inn, filled with so many of her friends and family members. It gave her strength knowing everyone had come out to celebrate her landslide victory in the election. She wouldn't spoil the mood by having a complete breakdown in the middle of her party.

Griffin's mother took a deep breath. "But you should know—"

"How's my best girl doing?" Maggie's father was next to her suddenly, pulling her in close to his side. "You need anything, sweetheart? Hello, Jana."

Jana inclined her head. "Jim."

"I'm great, Dad," Maggie lied. She truly was happy that she'd been reelected. It was her chance to prove she deserved her position as Stonecreek's mayor.

"Your grandmother asked if you'd stop by her table. There's some inn guest she wants to introduce you to—owns a techie company of some kind."

"Let's go now," Maggie said quickly.

She glanced up to see her father's gaze lingering on Jana, who continued to finger the button of her blouse.

"Thanks again for stopping by," Maggie told her.

"Of course," Jana said tightly. "Nice to see you, Jim. Give me a call next week about that commission for the vineyard garden."

Maggie heard her father's sharp intake of breath, but then he smiled and nodded. "Will do."

They turned and headed for Grammy's table.

"Are you sure you won't talk to Griffin?" her father asked quietly. "He's left several messages in the past days asking me to have you contact him."

"I'm sorry," she said, "but no. Have you ever heard the term 'ghosting'?"

Her dad cringed. "I don't think that's what he meant to do."

"It's been almost two weeks since he left and suddenly he decides to call? Too bad. Now that the election is officially over, I have more than enough to keep me busy."

"Busy isn't the same thing as happy."

"Close enough," she told him. "I've moved on, Dad. There's no room for Griffin Stone in my life. He simply wasn't the one for me." She smiled under her father's scrutiny, keeping her eyes bright.

"I actually believe you mean that." He leaned in and kissed the top of her head. "Good for you, Mags."

Who was the master of the poker face now? "Let's go talk to Grammy's VIP guest before she grabs the mic to call me over."

"You know her so well."

Maggie moved forward, because what other choice did she have? And if the ache in her chest had become a familiar companion, no one else needed to know.

* * * * *

Don't miss the stunning conclusion to the
Maggie & Griffin trilogy:

A Stonecreek Christmas Reunion

Coming in November 2018!
And if you missed the first book,

Falling for the Wrong Brother

is available now wherever
Harlequin Special Edition books and
ebooks are sold.

SPECIAL EXCERPT FROM

HQN™

Turn the page for a sneak peek at New York Times
*bestselling author RaeAnne Thayne's next
heartwarming Haven Point romance,*
Season of Wonder,
available October 2018 from HQN Books!

*Dani Capelli and her daughters are
facing their first Christmas in Haven Point.
But Ruben Morales—the son of Dani's new boss—
is determined to give them a season of wonder!*

CHAPTER ONE

"THIS IS TOTALLY LAME. Why do we have to stay here and wait for you? We can walk home in, like, ten minutes."

Daniela Capelli drew in a deep breath and prayed for patience, something she seemed to be doing with increasing frequency these days when it came to her thirteen-year-old daughter. "It's starting to snow and already almost dark."

Silver rolled her eyes, something *she* did with increasing frequency these days. "So what? A little snow won't kill us. I would hardly even call that snow. We had way bigger storms than this back in Boston. Remember that big blizzard a few years ago, when school was closed for, like, a week?"

"I remember," her younger daughter, Mia, said, looking up from her coloring book at Dani's desk at the

Haven Point Veterinary Clinic. "I stayed home from preschool and I watched Anna and Elsa a thousand times, until you said your eardrums would explode if I played it one more time."

Dani could hear a bark from the front office that likely signaled the arrival of her next client and knew she didn't have time to stand here arguing with an obstinate teenager.

"Mia can't walk as fast as you can. You'll end up frustrated with her and you'll both be freezing before you make it home," she pointed out.

"So she can stay here and wait for you while I walk home. I just told Chelsea we could FaceTime about the new dress she bought and she can only do it for another hour before her dad comes to pick her up for his visitation."

"Why can't you FaceTime here? I only have two more patients to see. I'll be done in less than an hour, then we can all go home together. You can hang out in the waiting room with Mia, where the Wi-Fi signal is better."

Silver gave a huge put-upon sigh but picked up her backpack and stalked out of Dani's office toward the waiting room.

"Can I turn on the TV out there?" Mia asked as she gathered her papers and crayons. "I like the dog shows."

The veterinary clinic showed calming clips of animals on a big flat-screen TV set low to the ground for their clientele.

"After Silver's done with her phone call, okay?"

"She'll take *forever*," Mia predicted with a gloomy

look. "She always does when she's talking to Chelsea."

Dani fought to hide a smile. "Thanks for your patience, sweetie, with her and with me. Finish your math worksheet while you're here, then when we get home, you can watch what you want."

Both the Haven Point elementary and middle schools were within walking distance of the clinic and it had become a habit for Silver to walk to the elementary school and then walk with Mia to the clinic to spend a few hours until they could all go home together.

Of late, Silver had started to complain that she didn't want to pick her sister up at the elementary school every day, that she would rather they both just took their respective school buses home, where Silver could watch her sister without having to hang out at the boring veterinary clinic.

This working professional/single mother gig was *hard*, she thought as she ushered Mia to the waiting room. Then again, in most ways it was much easier than the veterinary student/single mother gig had been.

When they entered the comfortable waiting room—with its bright colors, pet-friendly benches and big fish tank—Mia faltered for a moment, then sidestepped behind Dani's back.

She saw instantly what had caused her daughter's nervous reaction. Funny. Dani felt the same way. She wanted to hide behind somebody, too.

The receptionist had given her the files with the dogs' names that were coming in for a checkup but hadn't mentioned their human was Ruben Morales. Her gorgeous next-door neighbor.

Dani's palms instantly itched and her stomach felt as if she'd accidentally swallowed a flock of butterflies.

"Deputy Morales," she said, then paused, hating the slightly breathless note in her voice.

What *was* it about the man that always made her so freaking nervous?

He was big, yes, at least six feet tall, with wide shoulders, tough muscles and a firm, don't-mess-with-me jawline.

It wasn't just that. Even without his uniform, the man exuded authority and power, which instantly raised her hackles and left her uneasy, something she found both frustrating and annoying about herself.

No matter how far she had come, how hard she had worked to make a life for her and her girls, she still sometimes felt like the troublesome foster kid from Queens.

She had done her best to avoid him in the months they had been in Haven Point, but that was next to impossible when they lived so close to each other—and when she was the intern in his father's veterinary practice.

"Hey, Doc," he said, flashing her an easy smile she didn't trust for a moment. It never quite reached his dark, long-lashed eyes, at least where she was concerned.

While she might be uncomfortable around Ruben Morales, his dogs were another story.

He held the leashes of both of them, a big, muscular Belgian shepherd and an incongruously paired little Chi-poo, and she reached down to pet both of them. They sniffed her and wagged happily, the big dog's tail nearly knocking over his small friend.

That was the thing she loved most about dogs. They were uncomplicated and generous with their affection, for the most part. They never looked at people with that subtle hint of suspicion, as if trying to uncover all their secrets.

"I wasn't expecting you," she admitted.

"Oh? I made an appointment. The boys both need checkups. Yukon needs his regular hip and eye check and Ollie is due for his shots."

She gave the dogs one more pat before she straightened and faced him, hoping his sharp cop eyes couldn't notice evidence of her accelerated pulse.

"Your father is still here every Monday and Friday afternoons. Maybe you should reschedule with him," she suggested. It was a faint hope, but a girl had to try.

"Why would I do that?"

"Maybe because he's your father and knows your dogs?"

"Dad is an excellent veterinarian. Agreed. But he's also semiretired and wants to be fully retired this time next year. As long as you plan to stick around in Haven Point, we will have to switch vets and start seeing you eventually. I figured we might as well start now."

He was checking her out. Not *her* her, but her skills as a veterinarian.

The implication was clear. She had been here three months, and it had become obvious during that time in their few interactions that Ruben Morales was extremely protective of his family. He had been polite enough when they had met previously, but always with a certain guardedness, as if he was afraid she planned to take the good name his hardworking father had built up over the years for the Haven Point Veterinary Clinic and drag it through the sludge at the bottom of Lake Haven.

Dani pushed away her instinctive prickly defensiveness, bred out of all those years in foster care when she felt as if she had no one else to count on—compounded by the difficult years after she married Tommy and had Silver, when she *really* had no one else in her corner.

She couldn't afford to offend Ruben. She didn't need his protective wariness to turn into full-on suspicion. With a little digging, Ruben could uncover things about her and her past that would ruin everything for her and her girls here.

She forced a professional smile. "It doesn't matter. Let's go back to a room and take a look at these guys. Girls, I'll be done shortly. Silver, keep an eye on your sister."

Her oldest nodded without looking up from her phone and with an inward sigh, Dani led the way to the largest of the exam rooms.

She stood at the door as he entered the room with the two dogs, then joined him inside and closed it behind her.

The large room seemed to shrink unnaturally and she paused inside for a moment, flustered and wishing she could escape. Dani gave herself a mental shake. She could handle being in the same room with the one man in Haven Point who left her breathless and unsteady.

All she had to do was focus on the reason he was here in the first place. His dogs.

She knelt to their level. "Hey there, guys. Who wants to go first?"

The Malinois wagged his tail again while his smaller counterpoint sniffed around her shoes, probably picking up the scents of all the other dogs she had seen that day.

"Ollie, I guess you're the winner today."

He yipped, his big ears that stuck straight out from his face quivering with excitement.

He was the funniest-looking dog, quirky and unique, with wisps of fur in odd places, spindly legs and a narrow Chihuahua face. She found him unbearably cute. With that face, she wouldn't ever be able to say no to him if he were hers.

"Can I give him a treat?" She always tried to ask permission first from her clients' humans.

"Only if you want him to be your best friend for life," Ruben said.

Despite her nerves, his deadpan voice sparked a smile, which widened when she gave the little dog one of the treats she always carried in the pocket of her lab coat. He slurped it up in one bite, then sat with a resigned sort of patience during the examination.

She was aware of Ruben watching her as she carefully examined the dog, but Dani did her best not to let his scrutiny fluster her.

She knew what she was doing, she reminded herself. She had worked so hard to be here, sacrificing all her time, energy and resources of the last decade to nothing else but her girls and her studies.

"Everything looks good," she said after checking out the dog and finding nothing unusual. "He seems like a healthy little guy. It says here he's about six or seven. So you haven't had him from birth?"

"No. Only about two years. He was a stray I picked up off the side of the road between here and Shelter Springs when I was on patrol one day. He was in a bad way, half-starved, fur matted. As small as he is, it's a wonder he wasn't picked off by a coyote or even one of the bigger hawks. He just needed a little TLC."

"You couldn't find his owner?"

"We ran ads and Dad checked with all his contacts at shelters and veterinary clinics from here to Boise with no luck. I had been fostering him while we looked, and to be honest, I kind of lost my heart to the little guy, and by then Yukon adored him so we decided to keep him."

She was such a sucker for animal lovers, especially those who rescued the vulnerable and lost ones.

And, no, she didn't need counseling to point out the parallels to her own life.

Regardless, she couldn't let herself be drawn to Ruben and risk doing something foolish. She had too much to lose here in Haven Point.

"What about Yukon here?" She knelt down to examine the bigger dog. In her experience, sometimes bigger dogs didn't like to be lifted and she wasn't sure if the beautiful Malinois fell into that category.

Ruben shrugged as he scooped Ollie onto his lap to keep the little Chi-poo from swooping in and stealing the treat she held out for the bigger dog. "You could say he was a rescue, too."

"Oh?"

"He was a K-9 officer down in Mountain Home. After his handler was killed in the line of duty, I guess he kind of went into a canine version of depression and wouldn't work with anyone else. I know that probably sounds crazy."

She scratched the dog's ears, touched by the bond that could build between handler and dog. "Not at all," she said briskly. "I've seen many dogs go into decline when their owners die. It's not uncommon."

"For a year or so, they tried to match him up with other officers, but things never quite gelled, for one reason or another, then his eyes started going. His previous handler who died was a good buddy of mine from the academy, and I couldn't let him go just anywhere."

"Retired police dogs don't always do well in civilian life. They can be aggressive with other dogs and sometimes people. Have you had any problems with that?"

"Not with Yukon. He's friendly. Aren't you, buddy? You're a good boy."

Dani could swear the dog grinned at his owner, his tongue lolling out.

Yukon was patient while she looked him over, especially as she maintained a steady supply of treats.

When she finished, she gave the dog a pat and stood. "Can I take a look at Ollie's ears one more time?"

"Sure. Help yourself."

He held the dog out and she reached for Ollie. As she did, the dog wriggled a little, and Dani's hands ended up brushing Ruben's chest. She froze at the accidental contact, a shiver rippling down her spine. She pinned her reaction on the undeniable fact that it had been entirely too long since she had touched a man, even accidentally.

She had to cut out this *fascination* or whatever it was immediately. Clean-cut, muscular cops were *not* her type, and the sooner she remembered that the better.

She focused on checking the ears of the little dog, gave him one more scratch and handed him back to Ruben. "That should do it. A clean bill of health. You obviously take good care of them."

He patted both dogs with an affectionate smile that did nothing to ease her nerves.

"My dad taught me well. I spent most of my youth helping out here at the clinic—cleaning cages, brushing coats, walking the occasional overnight boarder. Whatever grunt work he needed. He made all of us help."

"I can think of worse ways to earn a dime," she said.

The chance to work with animals would have been a dream opportunity for her, back when she had few bright spots in her world.

"So can I. I always loved animals."

She had to wonder why he didn't follow in his father's footsteps and become a vet. If he had, she probably wouldn't be here right now, as Frank Morales probably would have handed down his thriving practice to his own progeny.

Not that it was any of her business. Ruben certainly could follow any career path he wanted—as long as that path took him far away from her.

"Give me a moment to grab those medications and I'll be right back."

"No rush."

Out in the hall, she closed the door behind her and drew in a deep breath.

Get a grip, she chided herself. *He's just a hot-looking dude. Heaven knows you've had more than enough experience with those to last a lifetime.*

She went to the well-stocked medication dispensary, found what she needed and returned to the exam room.

Outside the door, she paused for only a moment to gather her composure before pushing it open. "Here are the pills for Ollie's nerves and a refill for Yukon's eyedrops," she said briskly. "Let me know if you have any questions—though if you do, you can certainly ask your father."

"Thanks." As he took them from her, his hands brushed hers again and sent a little spark of awareness shivering through her.

She was probably imagining the way his gaze sharpened, as if he had felt something odd, too.

"I can show you out. We're shorthanded today since the veterinary tech and the receptionist both needed to leave early."

"No problem. That's what I get for scheduling the last appointment of the day—though, again, I spent most of my youth here. I think we can find our way."

"It's fine. I'll show you out." She stood outside the door while he gathered the dogs' leashes, then led the way toward the front office.

AFTER THREE MONTHS, Ruben still couldn't get a bead on Dr. Daniela Capelli.

His next-door neighbor still seemed a complete enigma to him. By all reports from his father, she was a dedicated, earnest new veterinarian with a knack for solving difficult medical mysteries and a willingness to work hard. She seemed like a warm and loving mother, at least from the few times he had seen her interactions with her two girls, the uniquely named teenager Silver—who had, paradoxically, purple hair—and the sweet-as-Christmas-toffee Mia, who was probably about six.

He also couldn't deny she was beautiful, with slender features, striking green eyes, dark, glossy hair and a dusky skin tone that proclaimed her Italian heritage—as if her name didn't do the trick first.

He actually liked the trace of New York accent that slipped into her speech at times. It fitted her somehow, in a way he couldn't explain. Despite that, he couldn't deny that the few times he had interacted with more than a wave in passing, she was brusque, prickly and sometimes downright distant.

His father adored her and wouldn't listen to a negative thing about her.

You just have to get to know her, Frank had said the other night. He apparently didn't see how diligently Dani Capelli worked to keep anyone else from doing just that.

She wasn't unfriendly, only distant. She kept herself to herself. Did Dani have any idea how fascinated the people of Haven Point were with these new arrivals in their midst?

Or maybe that was just him.

As he followed her down the hall in her white lab coat, his dogs behaving themselves for once, Ruben told himself to forget about his stupid attraction to her.

When they walked into the clinic waiting room, they found her two girls there. The older one was texting on her phone while her sister did somersaults around the room.

Dani stopped in the doorway and seemed to swallow an exasperated sound. "Mia, honey, you're going to have dog hair all over you."

"I'm a snowball rolling down the hill," the girl said. "Can't you see me getting bigger and bigger and bigger?"

He could tell the moment the little girl spotted him and his dogs coming into the area behind her mother. She went still and then slowly rose to her feet, features shifting from gleeful to nervous.

Why was she so afraid of him?

"You make a very good snowball," he said, pitching his voice low and calm as his father had taught him to do with all skittish creatures. "I haven't seen anybody somersault that well in a long time."

She moved to her mother's side and buried her face in Dani's white coat—though he didn't miss the way she reached down to pet Ollie on her way.

"Hey again, Silver."

He knew the older girl from the middle school, where he served as the resource officer a few hours a week. He made it a point to learn all the students' names and tried to talk to them individually when he had the chance, in hopes that if they had a problem they would feel comfortable coming to him.

He had the impression that Silver was like her mother in many ways. Reserved, wary, slow to trust. It made him wonder just who had hurt them.

Don't miss Season of Wonder
by RaeAnne Thayne,
available October 2018
wherever HQN books and ebooks are sold!

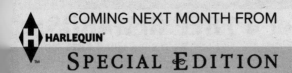

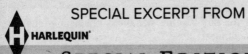
How hadn't he heard her first knock?

And then she saw the carrier on the chair next to him. He'd been rocking it.

"What on earth are you doing to that baby?" she exclaimed, nothing in mind but to rescue the child in obvious distress.

"Damned if I know," he said loudly enough to be heard over the noise. "I fed her, burped her, changed her. I've done everything they said to do, but she won't stop crying."

Tamara was already unbuckling the strap that held the crying infant in her seat. She was so tiny! Couldn't have been more than a few days old. There were no tears on her cheeks.

"There's nothing poking her. I checked," Collins said, not interfering as she lifted the baby from the seat, careful to support the little head.

It wasn't until that warm weight settled against her that Tamara realized what she'd done. She was holding a baby. Something she couldn't do.

She was going to pay. With a hellacious nightmare at the very least.

The baby's cries had stopped as soon as Tamara picked her up.

"What did you do?" Collins was there, practically touching her, he was standing so close.

"Nothing. I picked her up."

"There must've been some problem with the seat, after all…" He'd tossed the infant head support on the desk and was removing the washable cover.

"I'm guessing she just wanted to be held," Tamara said. What the hell was she doing?

Tearless crying generally meant anger, not physical distress.

And why did Flint Collins have a baby in his office?

She had to put the child down. But couldn't until he put the seat back together. The newborn's eyes were closed and she hiccuped and then sighed.

Clenching her lips for a second, Tamara looked away. "Babies need to be held almost as much as they need to be fed," she told him while she tried to understand what was going on.

He was checking the foam beneath the seat cover and the straps, too. He was fairly distraught himself.

Not what she would've predicted from a hard-core businessman possibly stealing from her father.

"Who is she?" she asked, figuring it was best to start at the bottom and work her way up to exposing him for the thief he probably was.

He straightened. Stared at the baby in her arms, his brown eyes softening and yet giving away a hint of what looked like fear at the same time. In that second she wished like hell that her father was wrong and Collins wouldn't turn out to be the one who was stealing from Owens Investments.

Don't miss
An Unexpected Christmas Baby *by Tara Taylor Quinn,*
available November 2018 wherever
Harlequin® Special Edition *books and ebooks are sold.*

www.Harlequin.com

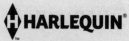

Love Harlequin romance?

DISCOVER.

Be the first to find out about promotions,
news and exclusive content!

f Facebook.com/HarlequinBooks

t Twitter.com/HarlequinBooks

O Instagram.com/HarlequinBooks

P Pinterest.com/HarlequinBooks

ReaderService.com

EXPLORE.

Sign up for the Harlequin e-newsletter and
download a free book from any series at
TryHarlequin.com.

CONNECT.

Join our Harlequin community to share
your thoughts and connect with other
romance readers!
Facebook.com/groups/HarlequinConnection

(H) HARLEQUIN®

**ROMANCE WHEN
YOU NEED IT**

HSOCIAL2018